SERPENT AND LILY

NIKOS KAZANTZAKIS

Serpent
and
Lily

A Novella,
with a Manifesto,

"The Sickness of the Age"

Translated, with Introduction and Notes, by
Theodora Vasils

UNIVERSITY OF CALIFORNIA PRESS
Berkeley   Los Angeles   London

University of California Press
Berkeley and Los Angeles, California
University of California Press, Ltd.
London, England

ISBN 0-520-03885-1
Library of Congress Catalog Card Number 78-68832
Copyright © 1980 by The Regents of the University of California

Printed in the United States of America

Acknowledgment is made to Simon and Schuster, Inc., for permission to quote from Nikos Kazantzakis, *Report to Greco,* copyright © 1965, pages 135-137. Acknowledgment is also made to Little, Brown and Company for permission to quote from *Journeying,* page. 3.

Contents

Acknowledgments   vii

Introduction   1

SERPENT AND LILY   19

     Chapter I   21
     Chapter II   34
     Chapter III   57
     Chapter IV   65

THE SICKNESS OF THE AGE   87

NOTES   103

     To Introduction   103
     To *Serpent and Lily*   106
     To *The Sickness of the Age*   111

SELECTED BIBLIOGRAPHY   113

     About the Author   117
     About the Translator   117

Acknowledgments

I acknowledge with gratitude my indebtedness to Helen Kazantzakis who presented me with the opportunity to make this work available to the English reading public. In preparing the English translation I have used the edition of the Greek text which was published in Athens in 1974 by Helen Kazantzakis. Also acknowledged is my indebtedness to Kimon Friar for his encouragement and advice; to the contemporary Greek writer, Elli Nezeriti, and Iro Athanasiades of Athens for their assistance in translating certain obscure words; and to my editor, John A. Miles, Jr., for his perceptive observations and recommendations. A debt of a special kind is owed my sister, Themi Vasils, who painstakingly read the complete manuscript and was ever ready and willing to confirm or correct, and to make crucial and invaluable suggestions.

Oak Park, Illinois   T. V.
December 1978

Introduction

This first work of Nikos Kazantzakis, together with his first essay, "The Sickness of the Age," which was published almost simultaneously with *Serpent and Lily* in the spring of 1906 and which is included in this edition as an illuminating companion piece, is particularly important in what it represents—the earliest source from which to trace the development of Kazantzakis as artist and thinker.

The work first appeared in Athens under the pseudonym Karma Nirvami, a pen name Kazantzakis frequently used in his early writings. In keeping with its erotic theme and the author's youthful verve, *Serpent and Lily* came out in a flamboyant red cover bearing the dedication "To my *Totó*," an endearing name for Galatea Alexiou with whom Kazantzakis was enamored and whom he later married.* The title page also bears the notation, "Mythistorema," a work of fiction.

As early as his student years at the University of Athens where he was studying law,[1] the young Cretan's writing created a stir among the literary elite of Athens. A year after the emergence of the bizarre *Serpent and Lily* Kazantzakis entered his first drama, *Day Is Breaking,* in a competition sponsored by the university and received a curious award from that institution. While bestowing its coveted laurel wreath upon him for the best of the plays submitted, the

---

*N. K. and Galatea were married in 1911 and divorced in 1926. Future references in this work to N. K.'s widow are to his second wife, Helen Samios Kazantzakis.

university's presiding professor denounced the drama's audacity and scandalous content. "We give the poet his laurel crown," he announced at the award-presentation ceremony, "but we dismiss him from these sacred precincts." Kazantzakis describes the incident in *Report to Greco:* "I was there in the great university auditorium, a beardless inexperienced student. Blushing to the ears I stood up, left the laurel crown on the judge's table, and walked out."[2]

When the Athenian journalist Vlasios Gavriilidis learned of the university incident he took up the cause of Kazantzakis in his newspaper *Akropolis.* "*Day Is Breaking,*" he wrote, "is a literary Theriso[3] as was also last year's work entitled *Serpent and Lily,* painted all in red, with a scattering of pages full of force and the south wind.... He enters our literary world bearing new daemons: intellectual, aesthetic, linguistic.... He is the new writer, the writer of fire and the writer of life."

Kazantzakis's emergence as the "new writer" was given further sanction by such critics as D. Kalogeropulos, the respected journalist and director of the periodical *Pinakothiki,* and the nationally renowned contemporary poet of Greece, Kostis Palamas, whose critique in the meritorious journal of the day, *Panathenea,* described *Serpent and Lily* as a "young artist's first fruits ... oozing with creative blood and the delirious fever of a creator's dream ... a poem youthful and sick, beautiful and morbid, moral and immoral." He predicted that Kazantzakis, in keeping with the investiture of art, would in time create the beautiful and healthy works that "uplift and cleanse the soul."

At the time Kazantzakis was writing *Serpent and Lily* his own soul was far from healthy and tranquil. He had just returned to Crete for the final summer of his student years and was tormented by the bitter aftertaste of an earlier amorous experience with a young woman whom he calls "the Irish lass" in *Report to Greco.* This young woman had given him English lessons, he tells us, during his student days at the gymnasium in Crete, and his first taste of sexual love, a love that he had blasphemously arranged to consummate in the tiny chapel at the summit of Psiloritis[4] on the eve of his departure from Crete to begin his university studies in Athens. Three years later he was still tormented by remorse and disillusionment. The young woman's door was closed to him, he had treated her badly after their tryst on Psiloritis. Now, filled with anguish over what he had done and failed to do, he roamed about the streets of Crete, an exiled Adam, returning again and again to the girl's house "as though he had committed a crime and was returning to circle about the victim." So profound was his anguish that he became physically ill with fever. One morning, without having any clear aim in mind or knowledge as to what he was about to do, he picked up his pen and began to write. Here is his account in *Report to Greco* of how *Serpent and Lily* was born:

... Perhaps if the anguish became embodied, if words gave it a body, I would see its face and, seeing it, no longer fear it. ... I began therefore to mobilize words, to regurgitate the poems, saints' legends, and novels I had read. . . . But the very first words I placed on paper astonished me. I had nothing like that in mind. I refused to write such a thing; why then had I written it? As though I had not been delivered permanently from my first sexual contact (yet I was certain I had been delivered), I began to crystallize a tale around the Irish girl, a tale full of passion and fanciful imaginings. Never had I spoken such tender words to her, never felt such raptures when I touched her as those I now proclaimed on paper. Lies, all lies, and yet as I enumerated these lies now on the sheet before me, I began to understand to my astonishment that I had indeed tasted great pleasure with her. Were they really true, then, all these lies? . . . Evidently there is a certainty which is more certain than certitude itself. But one of these is to be found a full story higher than that ground-level construction of humanity's which goes by the name of truth.

I finished in a few days. Gathering together the manuscript, I inscribed *Serpent and Lily* at its head in red Byzantine characters and, getting up, went to the window to take a deep breath. The Irish girl did not torment me now; she had left me in order to lie down on the paper and she could never detach herself from it again. I was saved!... I did not think of her any longer, except as I had refashioned and solidified her with words.... By means of imagination I had obliterated reality, and I felt relieved.

This struggle between reality and imagination, between God-the-Creator and man-the-creator, had momentarily intoxicated my heart. It pleased me, even if it meant my destruction, to wrestle with God. He took mud to create a world; I took words. He made men as we see them, crawling on the ground; I, with air and imagination, would fashion other men with more soul, men able to resist the ravages of time. While God's men died, mine would live!

Now I feel ashamed when I recall this satanic arrogance. But then I was young, and to be young means to undertake to demolish the world and to have the gall to wish to erect a new and better one in its place.

How Kazantzakis regarded this first work years later is not clear. We know that he omitted it, along with all his early writings, when compiling his final *complete works* which he began to publish in a special series in the last years of his life. We know also from the vivid description fifty years later in *Report to Greco* that he never forgot it. As late in his career as the mid-1940s, a decade before his death, he included it in at least two important lists of "collected works," once in the credentials that he submitted to the academicians of Athens when applying for a chair at the prestigious academy, and again a year later in his 1946 "collected works to date" which he compiled for the Nobel committee's consideration when he was nominated for the Nobel Prize.

It is the only early work that he has singled out for special mention in his final autobiographical summation *Report to Greco,* as if in recognition of the special rights of a firstborn. Certainly the language-conscious Kazantzakis, who labored and belabored a work, sometimes carrying it through several drafts in order to perfect the language, must have winced at some of the flawed phrases in this first piece. At the opening period of his career he was still writing in the obligatory (for students) *katharevousa,*[5] the purist language of the educated elite of the time. Though he experimented with a transitional modified demotic[6] style in *Serpent and Lily,* he still retained many puristic forms that are uncharacteristic of his later work. The mix of language, elegant katharevousa and earthy demotic, however, suits the tone of this early work which combines a decadent world weariness with pagan lushness. It is interesting to note that James Joyce, that other twentieth century Ulysses author with whom Kazantzakis is so often compared, shows a somewhat similar archaic style in his early letters to his wife Nora.

Despite the corrupting turn-of-the-century European influence,[7] that abhorrent ennui that the mature Kazantzakis later repudiated, flashes of the extraordinary Kazantzakis genius are already evident in this first work. But while the work has interest in its own right, it is mostly as a period piece and as a lesser stone in the larger monument that *Serpent and Lily* has particular merit. It is a valuable source of reference in tracing the author's development from his first adult steps and should be read in conjunction with his essay of the same period, "The Sickness of the Age." Published virtually together with *Serpent and Lily* in Athens in 1906, "The Sickness of the Age" outlines the familiar historical theory that is constant in Kazantzakis's writings and, in essence, points to the underlying "plot" in *Serpent and Lily.* The sweeping world view of this early work is even more impressive when one considers the author's youth. Primarily it deals with the plight of modern man caught in a transitional era, spanning man's history which begins with "the simplicity and joy of antiquity, through the devotion, ecstasy and faith of the Middle Ages, down to the licentiousness of thought of the Modern Age."[8]

In an essay entitled *Nikos Kazantzakis* (New York: Columbia University Press, 1972), Professor Peter Bien provides an excellent detailed analysis of this historical concept of Kazantzakis's which, he indicates, started with a theory of history and expanded to a theory of metahistory. The keystone of this historical thinking Professor Bien calls Kazantzakis's "doctrine of the transitional age." This doctrine holds that modern man is caught in the middle of a transitory period and can no longer respond to the beauties of this world with the simple spontaneous joy of his pagan forebears since Christianity has poisoned his appreciation of the physical world; nor can he take comfort in religion, since Science has destroyed his faith in a spiritual world.[9]

Kazantzakis's first nebulous attempt to aesthetisize this concept makes its shadowy appearance in *Serpent and Lily* where it is dramatized through the story's young hero, an artist and creator of sorts. We see the development of his historical concept in three stages, paralleling the corresponding historical epochs of man as outlined in "The Sickness of the Age." The opening stage shows the hero in his first encounter with Galatea the Beloved, who, we are told, came upon him one day while he was sitting on a park bench. "I fell in love with her, she fell in love with me—the eternal, the repetitious, the panharmonious song."

In the story's brief optimistic beginning Kazantzakis shows the young lovers reflecting the simple response to nature that is characteristic of the ancient world, a world he is nostalgically partial to in the companion essay. He depicts the hero matter-of-factly expecting love to come, and describes the encounter with words that evoke the power and

6

cyclical law of the seasons. "I was waiting for You like the frozen earth in its winter solitude.... You are Spring and I am the earth, the great wanton mother, who opens her loins and waits." In a poetic cadence straight out of the biblical Song of Songs the lover's declarations of passion evoke the forthright simplicity and candor of the ancient world "where love was still an instinct—guileless and wild and direct."[10]

But even in this early stage of innocence there is a hint of foreboding in the sensations the lover describes. The Beloved's lips "distill nectar and the Poison of great kisses." She is "lovely as sin and lovely as Death."[11] Almost from the very beginning the hero is presaging what Kazantzakis, in his essay "The Sickness of the Age" describes as the inflexible doom that bears down on man's soul, a soul that throughout the ages has played out nothing else but Sophocles' tragedy, *Oedipus Tyrannus:* Oedipus knows nothing. He is fortunate. But in time he wants to know who he is and begins to inquire, and to forebode, but does not stop. The soul in the second act of doubt probes deeper for the truth. In the third act it sees the light and is blinded. There is neither joy nor pleasure any longer. The excessive light blinded our souls.

In the parallel second stage of *Serpent and Lily,* Kazantzakis shows his hero sated with the pleasures of his Beloved, and yearning for something higher. No mystery remains about her that he has not known, except one. He has "probed her completely with the microscope of his dissolute soul," a soul that he believes has come from better worlds. "Even if my body surrenders completely and if it quivers all over under Your caresses," he tells her, "even if my body is baptized whole in the sweat of voluptuousness and passion, my brow will be dry, far from the celebration of the body." The joyous innocence, the sensual mysticism of the brief first stage make way for the spiritual mysticism of the second, where the hero, in Christian symbolism, describes the

7

chaste spirituality that now seduces him. Galatea the Beloved, whom he had once enshrined in his soul, is now replaced by the Holy Chalice "which shines in its depths and ignites all the longings of his flesh for the Great Holy Communion." But he finds the Chalice too is empty, and begins to forebode and to understand and, like Adam the banished king, "remembers some other Country and weeps the hopeless bitter weeping of the orphaned and the exiled."

The final stage of the drama shows the hero in half joyous, half mournful resignation to the cosmic force that pulls him toward the mystery and harmony of the great Silence. In this act of the hero's vaguely self-conscious and willing participation in death, Kazantzakis appears to be introducing intuitively what he later worked out philosophically into a cosmological principle based on the Bergsonian theory that all life, all the cosmos, is basically in transition from one void to another, and that death is something toward which the entire Universe is moving.

In his structured formulation of this world view in *The Saviors of God*,[12] Kazantzakis describes the Universe as perpetually evolving toward self-consciousness. From matter to rocks to plants to animals to man, from sensation to instinct to reason to self-consciousness, the Universe is constantly struggling upward, fighting to slough off the weight of stagnant matter, burning itself out in its evolutionary ascent toward self-illumination, the ultimate liberation. Man, too, he says, in his propulsion toward self-consciousness, must imitate the Universal rhythm in its struggle to fight stagnation, must enter heroically into collaboration with a Universe that is governed by a power that both wills its own making and unmaking. "We come from a dark abyss, we end in a dark abyss, and we call the luminous interval life."[13] Life, itself, Kazantzakis says in the same breath, is something that we sense is without beginning, an indestructible force of the Universe. In his definitive credo, *Spiritual*

Exercises, he describes it as the preexistent energy, the primordial essence or élan vital in the Universe that is one and the same with God. This God, or life force, he believes, wills itself into being alive through union with the two opposites that compose it—spirit and matter. In the process of creation, these two streams collide. The one, the male sperm of the Universe, surges upward toward composition, life, and immortality; the other, the female element, pushes downward toward decomposition, matter, death. Inertia, stagnation, and decay, the female attributes of the universal generative process, by necessity thwart the male creative urge that, by a necessity of its own, shoots upward. Thus the life force that wills itself into becoming alive through union, upon its consummation, wills its simultaneous unmaking—"at once the setting forth and the coming back."[14]

Kazantzakis views the world as a giant erotic arena, a battlefield in which two violent contrary winds, one masculine and the other feminine, eternally meet and clash at a crossroads "where, for a moment they counterbalance each other, thicken and become visible." He sees God and matter as husband and wife; the primordial pair that wrestles in the nuptial bed of flesh, spawning and filling sea, land, and air with species of plants, animals, men, and spirits. "God is imperiled in the sweet ecstasy and bitterness of flesh," he says in *Spiritual Exercises,* "but he shakes himself free, leaps out of brains and loins, then clings to new brains and new loins, until the struggle for liberation again breaks out from the beginning." It is man's highest duty to assist God in this struggle to transubstantiate flesh into spirit, and to burn himself out in the service of advancing life upward toward its evolutionary end.

The transubstantiation of flesh into spirit which the hero in *Serpent and Lily* has begun but does not consciously understand is, on an intuitive level, an introduction to what is central to all of Kazantzakis's work. His vague sense of peril, his struggle against the female's constricting pull toward earthly things, in a hazy way presages the "God is imperiled" theme in *Spiritual Exercises* which impose a duty on men to act as *saviors of God*. This is not to suggest that the ripened concept of the *Saviors of God* is readily evident in *Serpent and Lily*. What is evident is the beginning of the struggle to liberate spirit from flesh, the beginning of the struggle that engaged Kazantzakis's thinking throughout his life.

It has been suggested that what is uniquely distinctive in the work of Kazantzakis is his attempt to synthesize philosophy with art. His own awareness of the limitations of such a union are recorded at a fairly early stage in his career, in a conversation with his friend Manolis Georgiadis.[15] "My aim is not Art for Art's sake, but to find and express a new sense of life (remember Nietzsche and Tolstoy). In order for me to attain this aim there are three paths: (1) the path of Christ, but that is inaccessible; (2) the path of Saint Paul which combines Art (the Epistles) with Action, but a Christ is needed; (3) the path of Art or Philosophy (Tolstoy or Nietzsche). I am following the third, and that is why whatever I write will never be perfect from the point of view of Art. Because my intention transcends the limits of Art."[16]

In her biography the author's widow separates Kazantzakis's work into four periods. The first (1906-1918) she describes as a period of groping in which he experimented with his developing philosophical ideas in dramas and essays. Among his published writings during that period was a play entitled *Comedy* (1909), which dramatizes the plight of eleven dead men shut in a room with no exit, a striking forerunner of Sartre's *No Exit* which was written some thirty-five years later.

At the start of the second period (1918-1924), following the crucial years of World War I, Kazantzakis was still struggling to formulate his world view. The process is

10

described in a short philosophical work that he was writing at the time, entitled *Symposium,*[17] which curiously had found its way into his father's strongbox and was not published until long after the author's death when his nephew, Nikos Saklampanis, brought it to light some fourteen years later. By 1924 Kazantzakis had crystallized his thoughts and set down his formalized world view in the definitive philosopical work *Spiritual Exercises.* With the formulation of his theoretical credo behind him, Kazantzakis began once again to think of aestheticizing his concepts. More and more, his notes reveal, he was coming to believe that theories were ephemeral, and that the only things capable of resisting time were works of art.

The third period (1924-1942) finds him turning his thoughts in earnest to giving poetic form to the ideas he has developed. But once again he is confronted with the impossibility of ever expressing fully what is inexpressible. "The creator," he writes in the Prologue of his *Journeying,*[18] "wrestles with a hard, invisible essence that is superior to him. And the greatest victor emerges defeated because our deepest secret — the only one worth telling — always remains untold. It can never submit itself to the material boundary of Art . . . we see a tree in bloom, a woman, the star of Dawn, and we cry 'Ah,' and our heart can hold nothing more." It is this "Ah" that Kazantzakis despairs of ever converting into thought and art without reducing it to "brazen painted words full of empty air and fantasy." Yet he sees no other salvation for his ideas. He has nothing in his power, he declares, but twenty-four little lead soldiers with which to conquer Death.[19]

Death, the major adversary in Kazantzakis's life and work, is the formidable protagonist upon which he whets and hones his strengths. In pitching his battle, Kazantzakis has no illusion about the ultimate invincibility of life's adversary. But man's worth, he believes, lies not in victory

11

but in the *struggle,* in how courageously he lives and dies, without condescending to accept reward; and in something even more ennobling—in how valiantly he struggles in the full knowledge that no reward exists outside himself to imbue him with the joy, pride, and valor of his struggle.

During this period of world chaos, Kazantzakis was living in Germany, a defeated, anarchistic Germany. All Europe was in upheaval and flux from the devastating war and was heading insanely toward another even greater global conflict. His own country had just suffered a crushing and humiliating catastrophe in Asia Minor and, although Kazantzakis had by now begun to transcend the boundaries of nationalism, the Greek defeat on the eve of a long over-due era of hope for his "martyred" race affected his soul profoundly. To quiet his spirit and refresh his mind and body he returned to Crete where he would find solace in the mountains, and nourishment from the soil and ancient lore of his birthplace.[20] One day, wandering through the ruins of Knossos, his attention was arrested by the bullfight frescoes on the palace walls. It was as though he were seeing them for the first time; the graceful agile youths and maidens confronting the monstrous bull with discipline and valor, playing their cool measured strength against the bull's ferocious power like some exalted game, with artistry and grace, and proud intrepid glance. He felt a sudden affinity to these remote ancestors who had transubstantiated horror by turning it into a game, pitting their virtue against mindless omnipotence. The Cretans did not kill their bull as other civilizations killed their monsters. They did not look upon it with fear, as an enemy, but as a formidable protagonist on whom they honed their bodies and souls to make them strong and valiant. It was the symbol Kazantzakis had been looking for. From now on he would view the abyss with such an intrepid stance; he would fill the eyes of his Odysseus with just such a Cretan Glance.[21]

Having "discovered where to stand, and how to cast his gaze," Kazantzakis now turned his sights toward a new period of creation, toward bringing forth Odysseus who was ripening in his brain. Between intervals of travel, which were indispensable for the revitalizing of his spirit and body, he disciplined himself to long periods of harsh exile for the absolute freedom that he needed to create his *Odyssey*.[22] The severance of human contact that absolute freedom implied was not new to him. He was without a peer among his countrymen, and all his life he suffered the isolation of a man alone in his land. Solitude was his natural element and something that he sought out, but his letters during some of these periods of hermitic existence reveal moments of unspeakable loneliness—*alone with the alone*. His biographer Pandelis Prevelakis notes a telling passage from the *Odyssey* that Kazantzakis had begun to write shortly before he met the young Prevelakis: "In waste, in desolate waste, even a worm's shade is good."[23]

Much has been made of Kazantzakis's asceticism. In his *Study of the Poet and the Poem,* Prevelakis paints a picture of Kazantzakis in a setting much like that of the prophet Elijah, at the brook of Kerith where the prophet waited for the raven to bring him his daily bread. He describes a man absorbed only by the horizons; a man who gave no thought to embellishing his hermitage, nor even in working the strip of earth outside his door. For such a man, he writes, renunciation could not but include woman also. In truth, Kazantzakis struggled constantly to conquer triviality and to escape the ensnarement of the joys of everyday life. Like the prophets of the Old Testament he viewed women as distractions who sidetracked man's mind from an even higher joy. In this he shared the view of Thomas Mann, one of the first of his contemporaries to recognize his worth, who also scorned "Die Wonnen der Gewöhnlichkeit," or joys of mediocre domesticity that disrupt the creative mission of the superior man. But although Kazantzakis struggled against this enticement all his life, scourging the sensual side of his nature with periodic flights to monasteries and retreats into mountain solitude, he never fully repressed the erotic instinct.[24] Indeed, his notebooks reveal a man both attracted and attractive to women; a man who had no wish to detach himself completely from the feminine lure of beauty and human tenderness. We need only read his confession to his adopted "grandfather" in *Report to Greco*, and note specifically the poignant tribute (poetically idealized but nonetheless revealing) to his wife and helpmate of thirty-three years, to appreciate the profound affection and gratitude he felt for the women in his life.[25]

While embracing asceticism most of his life, Kazantzakis was not beyond enjoying physical comforts and pleasures in the most aristocratic sense. During a visit to England in July 1939, he describes with obvious appreciation the quiet wealth of the English squires in their ancient countryside castles. "We should have been born here," he writes to Prevelakis, "rich, silent, isolated squires like the lords I've met, living in distant English country districts, inside comfortable old castles, with the portraits of their ancestors. . . . When I die, some biographer of mine will write . . . that I was of an ascetic nature, with few desires, a man who thrived on living in deprivation. And no one will know that if I ended up an 'ascetic' it is only because I preferred nakedness to the cheap humiliating livery of the bourgeoisie."[26]

In attempting to analyze Kazantzakis in his *Study of the Poet and the Poem*, Prevelakis suggests that the surpassing of the erotic instinct is a theme in Kazantzakis's art that is most apt to feed and, indeed, to deceive psychoanalysis. "Man slaughters woman—in the literal and metaphorical sense—in order to dedicate himself completely to his Rule." Prevelakis describes the concept as beginning with *Serpent and Lily* when the hero "sets off the hecatomb" by compel-

14

ling his beloved to join him in committing suicide, having been driven mad by the incapacity of their souls to commune completely. A similar theme can be found in the writings of D'Annunzio who had profoundly influenced Kazantzakis as a youth, notably in his *Triumph of Death* whose character Giorgio Aurispa also had failed to penetrate the subconscious mind of his beloved. The theme, Prevelakis observes, continues almost without exception throughout Kazantzakis's works: in the *Masterbuilder,* the heroine is walled up alive in the foundation of the bridge, Tsimiskes sends Theophano to a nunnery,[27] Christ ignores the charms of the Magdalene,[28] Odysseus denies Penelope and Helen,[29] to name but a few.

The sacrifice of woman, Prevelakis continues, also has its counterpart in something else that is characteristic of Kazantzakis—the destruction of the sensible world by the poet. He seems to take a harsh pleasure in the godlike act of creating and obliterating the world. In this repeated act of creation and obliteration, Prevelakis asks, could Kazantzakis be expressing an ascetical renunciation? Was this to be interpreted as "an unsatisfied desire for communion, changed into vengeful nihilism?" Whatever the interpretation, this theme was from the beginning a familiar one in Kazantzakis's work, and may perhaps best be explained in terms not of nihilism but in the Nietzschean world view that Kazantzakis had been attracted to as a young man, a world view that imposed a duty on man to smash the old idols and create new ones.

Nowhere is the act of creation and sudden obliteration, and the dual tendencies of asceticism and sensualism in Kazantzakis's art more evident than in his epic poem the *Odyssey,* which he was writing during this third period. It is significant to note that for every act of erotic asceticism in which Kazantzakis shows man renouncing woman there is an equal and perhaps even stronger act of erotic affirma-

15

tion. While it is true that Odysseus ignores Penelope and Helen (both ancient loves) he goes on to conquer and enjoy new women, with all the zest for carnal gratification that his colossal sensual appetite demands. One need only refer to Kazantzakis's description in Book III of the *Odyssey* to see with what lyrical and life-affirming delight he describes Odysseus in the act of possessing an eager blackhaired maiden who welcomes his lustful embraces, thinking him a god who had come to her stream for water. These twin tendencies of asceticism and sensualism which flow through all of Kazantzakis's work are indicative of the dual vision[30] with which he views the world and partially explain the seeming anomalies in his thought and art.

In the context of his *ouevre,* Kazantzakis considered the *Odyssey,* which was written midway in his career, the most important of his works and the one for which he wanted most to be remembered. He believed he had created an archtype in Odysseus, a mold into which the man of the future might flow. As W. B. Stanford notes in *The Ulysses Theme,*[31] Kazantzakis's Odysseus is a fully integrated hero, both wanderer and politician, destroyer and preserver, sensualist and ascetic, soldier and philosopher, pragmatist and mystic, legislator and humorist. In fashioning his hero, Kazantzakis asserts, he was also fashioning himself, imbuing Odysseus with all of the virtues that he himself had striven for but had not been able to attain. As in his own life, he infused Odysseus with the dominant passion for freedom and the willingness to pay the price that absolute freedom demands: separation from one's fellow men. To symbolize this Kazantzakis sends his hero to the icy polar wastes at the end of his *Odyssey* to die. But unlike the embryonic hero in *Serpent and Lily,* who also sets out to confront death, in some vaguely prescient yearning for liberation, Odysseus embarks with boldness and full understanding for the desolation of the Antarctic, with none of the black pessimism that pervades the earlier novella. Unlike his first hero, Kazantzakis advances his Odyssean hero by stages to full maturity, and by the end of his life Odysseus understands the price of liberty and accepts it with cheerful valor. The arrogance that Kazantzakis was fond of attributing to his youthful endeavors may indeed have been tempered in maturity as he asserts,[32] but the sense of messianic duty that compelled him to want to assist in inching man's evolutionary process forward remained a constant motivating force in his art throughout his life.

With the completion of the *Odyssey,* amid a burst of creative energy that produced a prodigious array of major works that include the *Life and Times of Alexis Zorba,*[33] Kazantzakis entered his fourth and final period (1942-1957), the period of the great novels.

With the final novels, Kazantzakis's life comes full circle. Against a background of a world at war, and later of the fratricidal conflict in Greece when the very survival of his country was in question, Kazantzakis turned his gaze inward, to the earliest memories of the Crete of his childhood. Crete had never ceased to shape his life and thought. It had taught him where to stand and how to cast his gaze. The floodgates of this last period were in reality opened by *Zorba,* the first of the final novels to depart in style from the strident philosophical character that underscores so much of Kazantzakis's earlier work. This is not to say that the philosophical concepts that preoccupied him all his life are not present in the novels of this last period. The familiar themes are all there: the dark abyss, man confronting God, flesh versus spirit, the same world view, the same prophetic fervor. But the philosophical element is subordinated now to the artistic. Instinctively Kazantzakis turned to art, returning to his aesthetic nature and to his Greek roots to save both the vision of his country and his theories from oblivion.

The great novels of this period reflect the heroic affirmation of life in the face of the abyss that Kazantzakis had discovered on the walls of Knossos as a youth, and had come to understand as a man. His own life in these final years had achieved a serenity and calm that has been described by his widow Helen as having the scent almost of holiness about it. With the confidence partly of age and partly of knowing his strength, Kazantzakis, in maturity, had reconciled the enmity he had deliberately and by predisposition kept alive between flesh and spirit, the chasm that characterizes the struggle in the early hero of *Serpent and Lily*. Indeed, in his final work he had come to view the two deathless elements soul and body as friends, each capable of infusing the other with its own essential strength. Almost the last image that he left on the closing pages of his autobiography[34] is a picture of the bullfights at Knossos which depicts the perfection of this harmonious partnership of body and spirit and expresses, perhaps better than anything, Kazantzakis's vision of how man should play the exalted game of life, and how he should die.

Karma Nirvami

Serpent and Lily

To My *Totó*

I

May 2

I have a fever again today. Chills are coursing through my
body—something is wrenching and stretching in my mind—
as though a spring were suddenly jerking loose—as though
an untamable thought were violently unwinding behind my
forehead.

The fragrance of her body is still lingering about me
slowly dying, seeping through my flesh and intoxicating my
soul. Someone is pushing me to run after her; to tell her to
come back and sit on my knees and give her lips to me again.

I see those red lips like two big drops of blood and when I
bend over them to kiss them a wild passion and an instinct
from a primitive cannibalistic age rumble through my veins
—and I shiver—as though I were sucking on human flesh
dripping blood.

May 3

Today I am somewhat calmer. She will not be coming this
evening. I long for her and fear her. It is strange what I feel
for her, for that lissome body and those enormous eyes and
those red, those blood-drenched lips.

One night, in a dejected mood I sat down in a garden outside of town. I had the feeling that my soul was waiting for
someone. I turned my head and saw her. She was smiling

and lovely as she approached beneath the trees. A hand pushed me. O how I remember it; an omnipotent hand pushed me. And I approached her and told her my name — a well-known artist's name — and asked her if she would allow me to sketch her.

I fell in love with her, she fell in love with me. The eternal, the repetitious, the panharmonious song!

And now I want this body with the enormous eyes and the blood-drenched lips to keep coming, to keep bending over me, to keep filling my room with the intoxication and terror of bliss. To keep paralyzing my nerves and keep draining my body with that enervating and deadly caress of desire. I feel a pain, for days on end, in the places where she kisses me — like a burn. A poisonous sweetness trickles from her lips into mine and paralyzes all my reason and all my flesh.

When she leaves and I turn to my painting again, weird outlandish designs leap from my hand, licentious unions of lights and shadows and delirious frenzied colors. Infinite motionless seas, clouds with queer shapes that race across the sky and descend on the horizon and darken freakish gigantic suns that are setting . . .

May 5

You ventured into my soul and I knew You would come. I was waiting for You. I was waiting for You like the frozen earth in its winter solitude aches and waits. You are Spring and You come gently, O so gently pushing forward into my soul. My thoughts unfold and blossom and grow fragrant in Your path. The hue of hope sprouts and smiles beneath Your feet. Your breath, warm and comforting, passes over my soul and my dreams waken from the torpor of their passionless winters and they see You without surprise and they smile at You. They knew You would come. Some birds inside me open their eyes and flap their wings. And You smile and push forward O so gently, queen within my soul.

Gently, gently, You push forward in my soul with the roses' haughty pride and the boundless ivy's longing and the bashful violets' silent plea. And a kiss without end tinglingly spreads and quivers across my body. I sense it—You are Spring, Exquisite and Blessed One, and I am the earth, the great wanton mother—who opens her loins and waits.

May 10

Come . . . a secret nostalgia saps my soul and a chaste longing roosts in the great marble temple and pulls at me. Come with me. We will lie together under the marblized harmony, we will join hands and the sinful city will stretch out below us and we will watch how the violets shed their petals in the sunset on the waters beyond.

The violets shed their petals in the sunset and the colors revel down there. O Most Beloved! my knees are limp with desire and kisses revel on my lips. The joy of life rolls all powerful in my breast. And Love regales my soul with the mystical wine of spring and delirium.

O Most Beloved, my love is celebrating tonight. Look at the gay and boisterous holy procession ascending from Kerameikos[1] and approaching—like a wave that surges with song and rises enamored to kiss the beautiful cliffs.

O Beloved, O Goddess, rise upon the marble and smile. I am celebrating the great Panathenaea of my love. And those are my dreams dressed in their holiday finery that have set out from the cemetery to pass through the Double Gates[2] and slowly ascend the Sacred Rock.[3] They hold the precious artfully woven Sacred Veil in their hands. Day and night my thoughts—lovestruck laborers—were bent over it, embroidering. They were bent over it by night under the moon's magic and by day in the sun's flaming love, embroidering.

O Beloved, O Goddess, rise upon the marble and smile. Nike[4] rests in Your hand. Your body is of ivory and glows in the night. And at Your feet the great serpent lies coiled in a heap—that subterranean God who scatters the riches from the depths of the earth. The pillars are rising proudly and the stark white bloom of the marble is taking on life and all the Gods are returning again to the frieze and the war of the Lapiths and Centaurs is once more being waged on the metopes.[5]

Smile on the orphaned pediment, O Life and Love, and the marble thoughts of Phidias[6] will return once more and the Virgin Goddess will issue fully armed and the Gods will assemble smiling.

The triglyphs and friezes are regaining their youth and the roof spreads over them and the sleeping colors waken and our exiled statues return joyous and all-beautiful and walk up to their pedestals, their stark white limbs moving tranquilly within the marble and artistic lines.

O Beloved, O Goddess, rise upon the marble and spire Intact in the depths of the shrine and smile. The procession now ascends the marble steps to fall at Your feet and worship You. My black forebodings, my degenerate passions, my brooding thoughts all drag themselves tethered across Your altar to be sacrificed. My longings race to Your temple like horsemen, O Greatly Beloved, and my yearnings, unconquerable virgins, cross the Propylaea like basket bearers[7] carrying red wild flowers that they gathered in heaps from the licentious fecundity of my heart.

You are the only Goddess, You are Truth and Victory! Eternity smiles on Your brow and the ardor of life kindles on Your lips and all the cabalistic and shameful aspects of love

24

bring a blush to Your cheeks. You are Rhythmic Harmony, You are Truth and Life. The holy procession of my love surges like a wave and spreads out beneath the Parthenon and my desires kneel and silently shed all their flower petals at Your feet.

Come, O Infatuation of my soul! descend from the marble and give me Your lips and give me Your body. The yearnings of the ages spill over the pillar tops and the desires of the dead generations leap from the soil. Deep in the white marbles' quietus the flaming red passion of life is igniting and taking possession of me.

In the murky light of dusk there beyond the waters of Salamis,[8] out of the soil of Kerameikos, the mighty memories majestically ascend the Sacred Rock. Come. I am celebrating the Great Panathenaea of my love tonight.

Let us fill our hearts, like Panathenaic cups, with the undiluted wine of the Ideal and our eyes will shine with the drunkenness of life and our lips will fill with kisses. And from this rock let us sing together of the beauty of Apollo and the vine of Dionysos and the broad brow of Athena and the eternal youthfulness of Hebe[9] and the red lips of Aphrodite, the eternally kissed and eternally thirsty.

Let us intoxicate ourselves on the boundless smile of our sky and the erotic unions of our earth's colors, on the songs of Kolonos's nightingales[10] and on the golden sun-rayed honey of our Hymettos.[11]

Come. Like the immortal Gods on the frieze let us, too, recline here on the marble across from Salamis that sallies from the sea like a gigantic triumph and smiles at us. . . . Let our hearts unfold like rosebuds, like vinaigrettes, like lips in prayer, and let them thank the mighty gods for creating life so beautiful and Your lips so red and my love so great.

Let Socrates and Alcibiades, Phidias and Diotima, Pericles and Aspasia, those mighty priests and priestesses of the

Beautiful, begin the dance and the songs and the liturgy. And let the Chosen People of the gods—all the Athenians and their ladies—join merrily in unison the joyous refrain of the Priests. And let all the flowers blossom round about, and all the harmony and rumble of the sea soar up to here and all the exiled calm and joy of Olympos return once more and spill down from the crowned columns of the Parthenon and from the gowns of the Karyatides,[12] and in the shapely limbs of the Athenian ladies and on the brow of the men let there mesh—that mighty, that holy Shudder of love.

May 11

O Your still body reclining on the white sheets and Your loosened hair on the pillow and Your pale lips that wanted to say something and could not!

May 15

All the fibers of my body were kissing and loving inside me. And when I clasped You to me with all the triumph of my desires while some God was smiling upon us there in the hollow of the bed, and bound myself to You ever so tightly, and heard Your eyelashes fluttering and agonizing under my lips, I sensed that I had captured the everlasting Chimera—that quivering in my arms, a prisoner, was the happiness and eternalness of the great chilling terrors.

I looked at You and You were pale and lovely and mysterious. And I knelt before You there in the hollow of the bed and joined my hands over the weariness and paleness of Your body, O Priestess of Voluptuousness and Love, O Creator of moments Eternal!

26

And I sensed some mystery being solemnized inside You. A brilliance was spilling from Your closed eyes and a phosphorescence was licking and carressing your thighs. And I said: You alone, O Priestess of Passion and Oblivion, can comfort and deaden my soul.

"Thy two breasts are like two fawns, twins of a gazelle feeding among the lilies until the day breathes and the shadows flee.... How fair are Thy breasts, my sister, how much better Thy breasts than wine, and the scent of Thy garments than all perfumes. Thy lips distill nectar, my bride, honey and milk are under Thy tongue, and the scent of Thy garments is like the scent of Lebanon. A garden locked is my sister, my bride. A garden locked, a fountain sealed. A pomegranate paradise with choicest fruits, henna with nard, nard and saffron, calamus and cinnamon, with all the woods of Lebanon, myrrh and aloes, with all the finest spices. Awake, O north wind, come O south wind and breathe upon my garden and let my perfumes flow. Let my beloved come to his garden and eat its choice fruit."[13]

June 3

I have a fever. I am suffering. Here, here in my breast. I feel a flame racing and bubbling in my veins. I have the feeling that if I were to open one of my arteries and let some blood flow, I should be relieved.

June 4

I want to plait flowers in my hair. And pile roses and apples and perfumes about me. And lay all my love upon them.

A vine of greenest ivy is lusting inside me, weaving round and round my mind, seeking some world to embrace. A mystical blooming of roses and violets is taking place inside me and I hear the buds sprouting and the shoots' eyes opening and the birds warbling, warbling. . . .

Some mystery is being solemnized in me. Some Ritual. I bend down and hear hymns and prayers in my breast and the flapping of wings that are opening and heartbeats that, like echoes of a phantom churchbell, invite my thoughts to the liturgy.

I feel a God descending in me. The spirit of creation is blowing over my thoughts and a finger trickling with light is touching my brow. A Raphael and a Praxiteles are working in me. I hear the brush, soft and almighty, scraping against my heart and I feel the great paintings unfolding and coming to life. Madonnas with gentle smiles and incomparable charms. Cherubs, with eyes like flowers, resting their golden heads on their arms and looking in hushed silence at the heavens.

I feel a mysterious chisel sculpting inside me and a miraculous hand moving up and down deifying marble masses behind my brow. Marble apparitions of Gods are glowing in the depths of my soul, carnal dreams are coming to life, erotic loves are issuing forth, and the Cnidian Aphrodite,[14] like a fleshly flower of a lovelier world, rises out of the waves of my desires, tranquil and loose-girdled—and Praxiteles who is inside me falls to his knees, sees his Phryne[15] and smiles . . .

O if all my Desire could become a single kiss and come to You one night and kiss You whole!

My eyes cannot behold enough of her. She leans her head on my breast and shyly embraces my knees in silence. And I pat the crown of her hair the way a mother pats her child when she is lulling it to sleep. A prayer falls from my lips and gently meshes with her hair . . .

All through the night You glow in my heart with a holy miraculous brilliance and the halo of a transcendental world. Like God in the burning bush of Horeb.[16]

Your love, like a silvery caress of the moon, clothes my soul with tranquillity and light. When I look at You my knees yield under a weight, involuntarily my hands clasp themselves together and my entire soul opens before You — this is how the flower opens when the sun looks upon it.

I dissolve in prayer and ecstasy and my lips grow pale from singing Your praises. What I feel for You is a religion and I am moved by an urge to climb the towering mountains that talk secrets with the sky each morning at the hour when dawn, like love, reddens their crests — and kneel before You and invoke You.

I see You rising before me like an exotic flower of some gorgeous fleshly bloom. Your lissome body knows the secret of the ivy's intertwining. And when You walk and when You bend over me and when You part Your lips and close Your eyes and when You surrender Yourself, it is a song, and the meshing of Your contours is music. The mysteries of eternal Desires hide in Your embrace and the enigma of the seas cruises in Your eyes.

And from Your lips there drips and drips the Poison of great kisses. The Lodestars' mysterious pull leaps from You and pours out of Your body.

I see You before me, in the desert of my life, rising like a palm tree nourished by the warmth of my longings.

You are lovely. Lovely as sin and lovely as Death. My Desire clothes You, O Longveiled Love, from Your white throat to Your breasts to Your loins where it entwines itself tightly and imprisons Your thighs and trails down to Your feet.

I see You coming, tightly clothed in my yearnings, gently and so lightly, like a dream afraid of waking. You come slowly, slowly — and I put my hand before me to cover my eyes — O vision's delight! — to see You better.

June 20

What, pray, is that fragrance that leaps drunk and riotous from inside Your body? When I bend over You I feel as though a piece of Your flesh is evaporating and entering my own — and that I am partaking of holy communion. And my thoughts get drunk and my innermost desires speak out boldly.

It envelops You like incense and sings Your praises, O my Love and my Goddess — You hold delirium imprisoned in Your flesh and exude its mystery. I bend over You and see worlds incomparable and worlds past — and longing throbs stronger the older they grow and disappear. I am in one of Astarte's[17] temples and incense is burning in the altars and perfumes are kissing the unchaste statue with the plethoric breasts.

And I trod upon fragrant plants and lose myself in thickets of cedar and ivy and hear the murmur of the Great Goddess' sacred birds—and everywhere, everywhere, beneath the foliage, within the domes of the temples round the statue of the Pandemos Aphrodite,[18] the eyes of my soul see beautiful sunburned priestesses with full painted lips, a golden diadem round their hair, the sacred bird in hand, waiting and smiling . . .

June 21

When You open Your enormous eyes and look at me, remote and harborless seas greedy for the sailor's body open before me.

Secret dragnets that inveigle ships, deep waters that exist and are replenished by mothers' tears. Waves that devour and capsize and dash the enormous love-struck rocks to pieces with songs and caresses and voluptuous curves. Deep waters that smile at their hapless victims while echoing the eternal, the deadly songs of love beside them.

When You open Your enormous eyes and look at me a magnet, a secret magnet, pulls me toward them and a voice full of harmony sweetly sings to me. And I, shipwrecked sailor of love, feel the urge to crawl into Your embrace, O Lorelei of souls! and drown in the liquid convulution of Your waves.

June 22

Your enormous langorous eyes glow before me day and night and guide me. They shine on love's footpath and illumine the walk of life with their sweet light. The sun passes over me and burns out in the waters. The stars bloom at night in the secret garden of heaven—but they shed and disappear in the darkness, and I stretch my soul on Your body and am pulled along with agony and mute joy in the great mysteries of Your eyes that kindle before me and lead me in the night.

Their rays slip in my hair and gently kiss my brow and spill inside me like luminous caresses. And my entire soul is cleansed and the waves of my desires are hushed and all my soul melts in an azure cloudless heaven—and glowing night and day upon it, trembling like two unwaning stars of love, are those enormous, those beautiful, those languorous eyes.

June 30

You are the only woman who has filled my soul. When You pass Your hand slowly over my hair, hidden worlds open inside me and a mystical flowering of lilies and roses and ivy blossom and weave round my thoughts. I feel the urge to stoop and scatter wreaths and roses and ingenious desires and secrets of love in Your path. When the memory of You dawns and casts its rosy hue upon my soul I see You emerging through the forest of my yearnings, along the mountain ranges of my passions, through the dense foliage of my desires, graceful, silent and with overflowing charm, and my dreams fall prostrate to their knees and watch You. You pass like light over my soul. And all my senses quietly join hands in worship at Your passing.

July 15

I am sitting in my studio before the paintings I've begun and cannot finish—sitting here, pondering. I'm awake and dreaming. And I see my Love approaching, smiling and soundless, with those enormous eyes and that white unwrinkled brow that has never been kissed and never been soiled by the caterpillar of contemplation. I have strewn her path with my happiness and joy and the lilies of my innocence and the holy flowers of the lotus. And she tramples them and kills them and approaches soundless and smiling upon my soul. And I shudder all over with love, with fear. My happiness and joy and the lilies are dying underfoot. And I hear her lips like burning steel pressing on my hair.

And the poison of desire ignites my blood. O my Chosen One! When I die I shall die of love and fear one night at midnight in Your embrace!

II

She came tonight smiling and joyful and took me for a walk. It was night and the houses were beginning to sleep. Family men were returning home with their wives, solemn and silent.... Young men, pallid from wakefulness, were heading slowly and dolefully toward some amusement. Now and then the rumble of a passing carriage could be heard. As for us, we were walking quickly—without speaking. I did not, nor could I, while in the midst of all those banal encounters with life, want to speak to Her.

Out by the sea we sat down on a rock. Something heavy was weighing on our breasts. Dense black clouds were hanging over us. Mournful, as though filled with tears. We were restless, both of us. Some premonition perhaps. We could not sit still in one spot. We kept pacing back and forth on the sandy beach, dumb mutes. The infinite sea before us. As though some infinite night were rising over the waters— some infinite sorrow.

We turned back wordless and sad. When we parted and I bent over her eyes and saw all my agony—and saw an infinite night, an infinite sorrow—I felt something wounded and beautiful droop in me and begin to weep.

I am restless. A weariness has imprisoned my body and my entire soul. I sit down to work and my hand drops exhausted and my eyes close and I fall to thinking . . . Yes, now I make sense of it, yes, a mystery and pallor of obscure misfortune hovers over her and licks her body. When I first knelt before her down in the garden it was night and we were alone and I shivered with fear and love. The trees were sighing all about and I could see the roses in front of us shedding their withered petals. Yes, some calamity was lying there in ambush. She was beautiful, tranquil, quiet. Her eyes looked like two live violets in the night. Her white body swayed like a huge lily blossom, virginal and innocent. The pollen of the flowers was reveling among the leaves. And when I knelt before her a voice of someone wounded and on the verge of death broke out of my heart, rose tearing through my breast and flung upon my lips the eternal pain of the eternal words: I love you.

A terror spilled into the garden and the roses' lamentation resonated in my heart. Something broke inside me. And when, O Doomed One, You turned Your lips and body over to the wild caresses of my desires and when You rolled stark white among the defoliated roses, no? didn't You see something? O Doomed One! now I understand. The evil daemon of night reared erect and stretched his mighty wings out there in the black mystery of the foliage, and the hissing, foul and deadly laugh that issued from his lips broke over us and filled the garden.

And I leaned over and watched You lying pale and happy on the dead roses. And You stretched Your arms around my neck and I felt a certain power, a certain destiny pulling me tethered, powerless and happy, a victim of Pain and love, out there in the mystical foliage beneath the black wings.

No, there must be an end to this. My mind is stretching to
the breaking point and I am fearful. Fearful of the gigantic
battle raging behind my forehead. Now when she comes I
shall unravel the mystery. The two of us will be alone, no
one will hear us. It will be night and I will draw her head
near the light and I will see. What manner of ships are roving in those seas and why are they bringing heavily laden
sorrows to my soul? I want to see. I will cover her lips with
my hand to keep from looking at them. I'm afraid to look at
them. I'm afraid for her. I will hide her forehead and her
hair and I will cover her body completely with mine and I
will leave only her eyes open and I'll bend over and see. O
there must be and end to this! I'm afraid I shall go mad.
This morning I sat down to work and a sketch of a woman
issued from my hand and unfolded across the canvas and a
red poppy like a huge drop of blood found itself painted on
her breast. Like a wound.

She came. Lovely and shy and comforting. Her lips were
red, not like blood, but like a partly opened rose that seemingly smiles at the wayfarer in greeting. Her eyes were soft
like velvet and my soul reclined on them and rested. And
when her hand caressed my brow my thought grew calm, it
ceased to howl—it submitted to the all-powerful all-white
little hand and smiled. She parted her lips. It was as if a rose
were speaking.

Did I work today? No my love, I was thinking of You. And
I hastened to cover the morning's sketch so she would not see

it. What does this have to do with Her? I fell at her knees, drew her head down and sang her my love. A serenely tranquil love, like clear water rolling in the verdure's peaceful down. A deadliness—a calmness like a gentle prelude to the bliss of death flowed inside me. I couldn't think. My heart was singing of love without my comprehending what it was saying, like an organ apart from me—like a spring I had touched and triggered into playing.

She was listening and smiling. I was listening, too, and was jealous of such love, such serenity and deadly stillness in love. When the piece was over and the silence began and the shadows intruded themselves more densely into the room I saw her bending over me mute and happy, and her lips glued themselves to mine—like two strange and blood-filled leeches that suck on souls.

A madness, a poison spilled over my body and I grabbed her and felt the softness of her breasts over mine—and her whole body shivered and yielded—and when we parted tired and happy and speechless and I was alone, an infinite pain welled up in me—as though I had nothing more to hope for and take pleasure in—as though I were alone, alone in the night . . .

August 4

O the mystical agony and thrashing of Your body on the sheets! You suffered the agony of sacrificial victims dragged to the altar. And the waters of eternal desires swooned in Your eyes.

Our kisses were shivers of premonition and deathgasps of delight, a harmonious cascading of all our bliss and the inconsolable lamentation of all my dreams.

I pace back and forth like a madman in my studio. Again the ghostly outlines and the chrysanthemums and the drops of blood leap in orgiastic frenzy beneath my hand. It is impossible for me to work. I cannot compose or create anything logical. Yesterday I started to paint Her and I sketched her body as I had seen it sprawled on the ground the previous night—and when I finished, I saw—I had drawn a huge lily that had been cut and thrown pitilessly into a strange profusely winding river. And today I see—it is not a river but a huge profusely winding serpent running about somewhere out there holding a beautiful enormous lily in its mouth.

O the miracle of Your flesh lying gorgeous across the bed! And Your heavy lids weighted down with desires! O the dazzling glow of Your body in the dark!

I wish I could pluck rose petals and cypress branches and pile flowers and prayers and lamentations in a heap and throw You on them! And be eternally stooping over You, my Dead Love, pouring my soul on your unplaited hair. As I look at You again tonight, weary and ravishing and still, I clasp my hands above You and pray to the great Power that kills. That she have compassion and mercy for us—for us poor luckless ones who love—and send us, now that You are pale, still and weary, the Great Comforter, the brother of Love, that eternal Joy and that eternal Calm.

You sleep and smile . . . I bend over You and see beneath the pallor of Your eyelids, behind Your long lashes, Your eyes still moist from pleasure's splendor and nostalgia. The kisses' cantharis ripples and shivers on Your lips, O Insatiable One, and an enormous wave swells and heaves on Your breasts, a wave of flesh that rages in the secret tempest of voluptuousness.

I clasp You tightly and the wave writhes imprisoned in my arms, it billows under my lips and covers me all over in an endless downy caress, as if seeking to capsize some ship, as if trying to capsize something and depart.

You sleep and smile. I have the urge to grasp You by the hair and put my hand on that swelling that keeps rising and falling at Your throat, and squeeze it and enjoy Your Pain, O Most Beloved, and see how Your eyes will open suddenly with fright and what color terror will impart to them, and what You will do with Your lips. I will squeeze You with both my hands on that swelling that keeps rising and falling at Your throat and I will see how beautifully the sinuousness of Your body will curve and twist itself about me. Your eyes will bulge and the agony in Your voice will be sheer pleasure —like the rattle of death, like those cries and curses that I sometimes hear in the night coming from the stars in their death throes. You will huddle in the corner of the bed and plead, and I will feel Your blood in my hands, O Wild Pleasure, trickling warm and soft through my fingers and splashing on the white sheets and dripping off the lace...

What's the matter with me? Why, nothing my love. Why am I pale? It must be from weariness and love. You were asleep and I was leaning over You watching You and smiling. O no, my voice isn't trembling... Why should it tremble my love? You were asleep and I was watching You and strange desires were igniting inside me to grab You with my lovesongs' wings and the omnipotence of my longings and go away, somewhere else my love, I don't know where... there where eternal joy rises out of still and secret waters. We will both lie down there speechless, beautiful and blessed. I will press my lips on Your lips and our kiss will be eternal and we will lie there on the earth and the nights will pass over us and the roses will shed and their petals will fall and our kiss will be unshaken, large as eternity and night.

You were asleep and I was scattering my lovesong on Your eyelids and Your closed lips.

O Most Beloved! don't cry, my love is wild and degenerate but it is eternal.

August 12

Don't cry. Don't cry . . . the wine of love — the wine of love intoxicated my soul.

August 15

I am pale and exhausted and still lying in bed trying to remember. Who, pray, was that angel who came in my dream last night and spread his wings over me and told me to wrestle with him?

I can still feel that powerful stranglehold round my body and the wounds that his hands seem to have scattered over me. I cannot move. Someone in the night cut off all the vigor of my youth. I am like a tree that has been lashed by rains and hailstorms throughout the night. Someone approached me in the dark and he had the merciless lust of triumph in his eyes, and on his hands he had the power that takes souls. And I fought desperately. I wanted to live and the desire of life made me a giant. O how viselike he grabbed me, that compassionless Angel who has no mercy, whose eyes glitter with the wild flashes of the victors! I still feel his savage breath like the piercing breaths of desert sands hot upon my lips, my lashes, my hair, my shoulders. And I reflect upon it now with agony and a shudder of dread.

Who, then, was that Angel who came to my dream in the night and spread his wings over me?

August 17

She came to my room tonight trembling and beautiful, with eyes reddened, most likely from crying. It was like watching a nightingale entering the hawk's nest. Compassion, love and compassion slipped inside me and softened my words. Why are you pale my love? No, You were not crying? Ah, You were entreating God on my behalf? A savage laugh tore through my heart. I said nothing. Ah, Doomed one, you should only know what I said to myself!

She brought me a bouquet of lilies. She held my head and kept silently pressing me tightly to her breasts, her lips whispering something. I am afraid it was a prayer. A heavy scent, warm and unchaste, was rising from her flesh and penetrating my body.

I told her to hush. I stripped the petals from the lilies and asked for her lips. I want the communion of Your body tonight. I long for the impenetrable and holy Sanctuary of Your flesh. As Minister of the True God I shall offer a sacrifice tonight and Your body will be the temple and our delirious ravings the hymns, and the languor after our pleasure will be an otherworldly religious ecstasy. I will partake of all Your movements and all Your undulations and all the mysteries of Your body. And when, exhausted, You lie back on the white sheets and Your arms tire of embracing I will come and kneel before You, O Holy Altar of voluptuousness —and I will join my hands and pray.

And later I will open Your eyes and there inside their azure depths I'll read the mystery that You keep hidden from me.

41

I kneel before You, O Chosen of my soul, and I beseech You.

Give me of the unmarred peace that sleeps and smiles upon Your brow and of Your movements' stately calm and of the moonlight that issues from Your chaste and tranquil soul like a nocturnal queen. I bow before Your silent eyes and I beseech You.

Where, pray, do all these people of serenity and silence hail from who cruise and smile in Your enormous eyes? I bend over them and watch. Your thoughts like tranquil lilies sway and ponder in their placid pools. Strange heavens without thunder and clouds, filled only with light and harmony —filled with God—are mirrored there and whisper to the waters of Your eyes. I can sense the enigma of happiness roosting there, and the mystery of peace that spills into the lakes at night when the light out there in the west dissolves and covers the waters. Large ships that have set out from other worlds laden with light and chaste songs and mystical lilies cruise in Your eyes. A white-clad angel stands on the prow with outstretched wings. He doesn't talk, he doesn't smile, but gently slips into Your soul and disappears—O endless Sea and O Tranquillity!

O don't close Your eyes when I kiss You. I want to see what the angels are saying at the moment You lower Your lashes laden with kisses, and how the ships capsize and break in the wild storm that the tempest of my desires raises in Your eyes.

O to love nothing, to hate nothing, to go far away from men and near the beasts—away into the wilderness. And there alone with my untameable soul confront the heavens. To strengthen my thought with the spectacle of the endless wilderness and to become an element of the tempest and a gust of the simoom and to unite with the silent spirit of the wilderness and baptize my soul by fire, in the colors that revel and carouse every night out there in the west.

O! to love nothing and to get my fill of the great nostalgia that my soul feels for the wilderness!

August 25, Morning

I am at peace, a serenity shrouds and softly envelops my soul. I went out into the forest to lie under the giant shades, to embrace mother earth, to forget. The giant trees over me and the mountains beyond were smothering my ego and negating my pain and my joy. I began to feel deep within me that I, too, am a part of all this forest, a trunk that thinks and walks and sprouts branches and sheds leaves and dies... A wave born of the river that runs, sometimes tearful and sometimes singing, down to the sea to die... Why should we be eternal? Why such egoists? Like some insects, we were born to kiss and die. Our dust scattered on the ground will nourish and become an element of the tree and of the rock and of the bird that sings and of the brook that weeps. Our thought likewise will become an element of the thought of other generations. And countless centuries will pass. And days will come when men will shiver with cold and they will huddle together and seek life and warmth deep in the hollows of the equator, and the last mother will give birth to the last child and the sobbing of humanity and the world will reverberate like a curse and won't even jar the other stars that will be orbiting calmly in the beautiful and all-smiling heavens. How ridiculous we are with our passions and our hatreds and our love! Now and then when I find myself sitting across a crowd of people, watching them walking by, I get the feeling that I am far away, watching from a great distance. A sparse din, a murmur of voices barely reaches me. And I see these beings coming and going proudly with head held high, loving and hating and fretting and laughing — and they're all running pell-mell toward an infinite silent insatiable pit. And I see them dropping one by one, their laughter breaking in midair — dropping like raindrops on the sea.

And lying under the giant shades in the forest I think to myself: How much more beautiful it would be if all these passions were to cease and if each man were to support his fellow creature, comforting him that he is alive, removing the obstacles along the way and pushing one another quietly and gently to the grave, happy and without pain. There peace is eternal. The murmur of kisses does not agitate our bones down there. Passions do not reach into the earth. The sea will still be singing its wily song and the trees above will be whispering and trembling in the air and they will still be blooming and they will still be sighing under the blows of the lumberjack. Man will be loving, and the beasts in the forests' depths will be groaning with love and hunger. Everything will be in flux and suffering and clamoring above us, and we alone, quiet and motionless, with folded hands will be under the earth waiting.

August 25, Midnight

What did She want? Why tonight when I was returning to my studio so tranquil should I find her smiling and lovely, full of fleshly delight, her lips swelling with myriad kisses?

Why should You come tonight when I was so dead?

Ah! You want kisses my love? You want kisses? Let us close the windows because I fear. I fear the stars that are laughing up there and dying and I fear the words that are spoken by the trees. Why am I pale? You want to know why I am pale my love? I am dead. I am just now returning from the tombs. And I've come to kiss You and take possession of You, all of You. Come, give me Your soul and give me Your lips so that I may poison them tonight. I will tell You the mysteries of the tombs and I will show You, O my chosen one, what the holes of those eyes see that look down in the earth day and night. Mad? You consider me mad? The earth is like glass and I see all the bones and all the corpses lying in the ground with folded hands, rotting. I have better eyes than You. Their foreheads are like crystal and I see the mechanism of their thoughts and all the springs and all the horror.

Do You understand me? No? O my love! I love You and I fear. I want You to give Yourself to me whole, whole, all Your past and Your present and all Your future, and let us join ourselves together and let me hide inside Your body and lose myself and not see. Not see that great shadow that sits over me and darkens my soul. Do You see? it's like a jet black wing that opens in a gigantic spread over our heads.

O hide me and warm me and kiss me, Doomed One, because I fear . . . because I fear . . .

August 26

Ah Doomed and innocent love, if You could see what I harbor in my heart! You left last night at midnight, happy and weary. I watched You inconsolable as You were leaving —I was at the window watching. I saw Your body whitely outlined in the night, I heard your footsteps softly die away and watched Your whiteness disappear.

I was inconsolable and when I lost You in the night I don't know why I went down to the garden and stripped the petals from the roses.

45

We are out walking together and she leans against me
trustingly and we return to the house together and close the
windows and the doors and put out the light and lower the
curtains and remain alone, all alone in the hollow of the bed
and I look into her eyes and grasp her by the waist and
watch her. And I find it strange that she doesn't scream and
doesn't call for help and that she doesn't die of fright there
on the sheets.

Ah Doomed One, haven't You understood yet who I am?
When we're alone in each other's arms don't You feel the
great premonition of Death over us? How can You be calm
and love? When I hold You tightly and ask for the mystery
of Your flesh and ask to slake my thirst—the thirst of my
soul more than my body—I can feel on Your lips and in the
quiverings of Your flesh the boundless desire of Death inside
You, rising and weeping inside me.

Something weeps in our kisses and a creaking of dead
bones resounds in our embraces and a dirge accompanies
the heartbeats of our love.

Something weeps inside me, Most Beloved, and beseeches
You. When You lie still and pale on the bed and close Your
eyes the better to enjoy, something weeps inside me and
beseeches You to close Your eyes and never waken.

The holy Altar of my soul shines in the depths of my most
secret and mysterious thoughts. There is where I've erected
Your idol, O Most Beloved. My dreams kneel ecstatically
before You and celebrate the liturgy. And my thoughts
ignite like tapers and melt at Your feet. My love plaits the

thorny wreath on Your head and my pain, boundless and fixed, is Your pedestal. My desires gasp dying at Your feet and the eager longing of all my body rises like incense round Your whiteness. Since the Moment I came to know You a mystical liturgy has been celebrating in my heart day and night. All my nerves and all my thoughts since then have learned to pray. And I kneel with my whole being before Your statue that stands and shines in the holy of holies of my soul, I kneel whole and pray to the mighty Gods, O Galatea![19] That you return to the dead stillness of marble, to eternal peace and eternal beauty—because I fear. A wave of sorrow is swelling and rising in my heart and groans and threatens all around You. A gigantic glut surrounds You.

O return, Galatea, to the marbled beauty of death before the wave engulfs You completely, before the wrinkles profane Your unmarred brow. I know a medicine that cures every pain, I know an immortal water that sates the thirst of anyone who drinks it. O my love, bend down from Your pedestal and come let me poison You with my lips, let me trickle the Great Desire into You drop by drop. The Great mourning and the Great Nostalgia of Nirvana where the beautiful is eternal and sleep is sweet and unmoving and the voluptuousness of Night is not poisoned by the bitterness of dawn.

O Galatea! All my thoughts and all my dreams and all the shivers of my body kneel before Your Idol—in the depths of my soul, and invoke Death.

September 6

Tell Your soul to kneel close to me and tell it to open its lips reverently and wait: The Angel of Pain holds the holy chalice of love in his hands and is traversing the worlds giving holy communion to souls.

I keep pacing back and forth, waiting for someone. I run to the outskirts of the city and climb the Hill and gaze before me and ponder. The sun is slipping slowly behind the mountain and all around it gold and crimson clouds are weaving the evening calm upon the waters. The dusk's serenity spills over the trees and kisses the cliffs and falls upon the sea and mountain crests in gentle sleep. The birds dally and spread their wings and lazily flit to their nests. The stars march out across the sky and smile, and simple souls look up at them and with the omnipotence of prayer they, too, open their wings and find nests up there in their rays.

Everything on earth is asleep and dreaming. I don't move so as not to waken the worlds of insects that are sleeping beneath my feet. Everything is hushed. Now the moon will come out over the mountain, pale and calm, and stand vigil over the slumber of her children like some anonymous mother's loving eye.

Everything is hushed. I sit on the hill and gaze before me and ponder. Night steals into my heart. And I ponder. And the peace of the Sea and the silence of the trees and the stars steal into my heart. And slowly, slowly I can feel the hopeless bliss of dead things entering and spreading inside me.

Come let us weep together. A wave is billowing within me —like a flood—and groans around You and implores You. A teardrop from my soul is billowing around You and implores You.

Come let us weep for those who cannot weep, who have dry eyes and tear-filled hearts. For the flowers that open and wither, for the mountains that are eternal, for the Gods who come and die on earth, for the broad brows and the broad wings with the tiny nests, for the stars that struggle to say something and cannot. Let us not kiss all night this time — only weep . . . The tears have been piling up on my soul for years and years now. And I am drowning. I am drowning, O Doomed One, O Beloved! Come, make me weep tonight in bed. Relieve my soul of the flood and of the pain.

September 16

The flower sags when given too much dew from heaven. My soul sags from love.

September 20

A flame is burning in me. Like a vigil light before the icon of God. And huge strange wings are spreading out before me, like the wings of a wild bird.

A claw is tearing at my heart. And huge mute droplets, like tears and like blood, drip one atop the other and pit my soul.

Don't cry and don't be frightened, Most Beloved. It's the great Eagle of Pain, it's the vigilant flame of Love. Don't cry — I smile at my Hurt and its wounds. My heart ruptures and I bleed inside. And night comes and You pass Your hand ever so lightly over my brow and the wings disappear and the bleeding stops — all the wounds heal and close in the night. God, envious up there, is taking vengeance. No, let us not weep — let us not condescend to weep! I feel something immortal in me burning and smiling. I have the same flame in me that He has and the same essence as the stars. Immortality rages inside me and so does the pleasure of Omnipotence and the great Kiss that world Creators harbor in their loins. Unbreakable chains bind me to the earth—but I feel Someone inside me who does not condescend to bow to God!

Last night as I was looking at her lying naked in the soft candlelight a savage desire bloodied my breast. I felt I had savored her entire being and no mystery remained about her that I had not defiled. Every part of her nakedness showed the bite of my kisses and the profane caresses of my hands and the serpentine form of my lascivious twisting body.

Eternal roads upon which my desire had trod. I felt I had savored her whole. Whole—only a single red mystery remained for me. It was hidden in there, under her skin, on her eyelids, in the snowy white swelling of her breasts—it was hidden in there and I could feel it flowing and reveling all-red in her veins.

And I knew I had not enjoyed her completely.

O! for her blood to spurt and spill on the sheets and her body to thrash on the bed and her eyes to fly open in terror and her arms to fling themselves round my neck with hope and fear!...

O the enchantment of blood!

And I smiled last night. O my Beloved, I will not die before I have enjoyed You completely.

I want to make haste to relish all of You. All the white mysteries of Your nakedness that lie sleeping and wait. I want to make haste, I may yet be in time to drain Your lips and all Your flesh and all the shivers that lie in wait in the depths of Your loins. Let no kiss be taken by Charon.[20] Let me take them all. I want to make haste because I feel we are dying, something is constantly sliding under our feet, a clock dial up there is advancing, ever advancing, and night is approaching. A magnet from the depths of the earth is dragging us, don't You feel it my Love? it is dragging us invincibly—in vain we grab at the flowers on the road to help us stand still. The flowers, uprooted lay dead in our hands and we continue to be dragged along. O my love, weave the triumphant whiteness of Your body tightly round me, clasp me even tighter, come—doomed are we who love —let us join our lips and our souls and our bodies with the great web of our desires, come weave Yourself round me, it may stop us a bit, some moments may pass without our being dragged down there, O! down there in the earth where an omnipotent magnet keeps dragging us. Come, let us hurry. Don't hold back a single mystery of Your flesh from me. I feel a soul—a Bacchante[21] inside me! Don't be afraid. Close Your eyes and give me Your hand and come let me show You all the untrodden paths of pleasure that I know. Wild the pollen of night will pass over us. And our kisses will rise all the way from our loins. Come, let us hurry. Someone is lurking in the corner of the bed. Some premonition is spreading out on the shroudlike sheets. O where can I flee and in what curve of Your body can I bury myself and how can I embrace You to keep myself from dying—to keep from dying before I enjoy You completely.

September 27

I gaze at You. And it seems to me—it seems to me, O Insatiable, O Woman, that if I scatter my love on the earth

51

the barren soil will grow fertile — and will conceive and give birth to myriad red roses and poppies and vines and ivy.

O how shall I look at You and how shall I curve Your body and how shall I scatter my longing onto Your ardent desire in order to seize the great voluptuousness that floats in Your eyes and slides down Your loins and spills silent and inviolate from Your thighs!

I long for Your body and when I crush it in my arms and it quivers and cries out with pain from the savage embrace a voice rises in me like a sob and my breast convulses with the despair and conviction that it is something else I am seeking. And so, pale, unsmiling and sad, I allow You to part from my body. And I bow my head and hear a sickle inside me mowing down strange things that are weeping. I kneaded and melded Your body completely in the flame of my desires and I gave it every undulation of licentious inspiration and every caress of nighttime's passions and clasped You to me and looked into Your eyes — I looked into Your eyes and said: My dream is You. And the voice rose inside me and a sob wrenched my heart.

O Most Beloved! No, no, I will never be in time to enjoy you completely.

And even if my body surrenders completely and if it quivers all over under Your caresses, Most Beloved, even if my body is baptized whole in the sweat of voluptuousness and passion — my brow will be dry, far from the celebration of the body, without pleasure and without surprise, unsmiling and sorrowful, sorrowful . . .

When she came last night smiling and gave me her hand and I looked at her eyes, we were alone, and visible through the half closed windows was the bloody struggle of the sun that was dying. What were the leaves saying down in the garden and why were the trees sighing and clasping their branches like despairing hands invoking Someone in the night? I looked into her eyes and smiled. Yes, every night You shall be drawn into my arms, O Doomed One, O Beloved! My eyes magnetize You and overpower You . . . I conquered You whole, I possessed all Your cells and all the hidden parts of Your nakedness. You are small and weak and You timidly crouch before me and beg for my kisses in order to live. You are small and weak and You cling to me at night and drink the poison of untamed passions that drip from my lips. Ah Doomed One! Don't You understand at last that I am that Magnet in the depths of the earth who drags You and murders and conquers You?

When my mouth swoons over Your body I pity Your poor lips and Your innocent eyes and Your white brow and Your breasts that only hold love. I pity all of You because I am defiling all of You—because I sense that my lips are profaned and are not washed by all those books that they have read, they're like caterpillars that kiss and sully the leaves of the lilies.

53

I stand and watch You. And I hate the whiteness of Your brow and the unfathomable innocence of Your eyes. You are white and You wound my eyes. And I want to stoop down mercilessly and let my soul pass over You and carve Your soul with furrows. I want to bloody Your heart with the blood of wounded and inconsolable hopes and with the incurable anguish of despairing thoughts.

You are white and wound my eyes!

And I want to crush You in my embrace night after night, and at dawn have You emerge unrecognizable and despairing, with an incurable wound in the area of Your heart and with that infinite lust for death in Your enormous, Your beautiful eyes. I want to be the one to shape Your thought and defile Your heart and spill Your soul into that dissolute womb that my soul has spilled into. I feel the power to corrupt You entirely in one night. To make You an echo of my pain, a creation of the corruption of my soul—a lily with evaporated fragrance and sullied bloom and broken petals, as if an endless squall had passed over it throughout the night.

October 6

O to have You wedged in the corner of the bed, stretched out across the sheets, and me closing the windows and letting down the curtains and stooping over You all night drinking Your soul! . . .

The lines of Your body yielded to my caresses and Your lips ran dry from the sucking of my lips. You yielded to me wholly and I desecrated all the mysteries and all the shivers and all the undulations of Your flesh. I sealed all the niches of Your body with the kiss of my desire. And the glut keeps rising, rising together with love.

I probed You completely with the microscope that my dissolute soul holds. I know what Your eyes say beneath their long lashes and what the squeeze of Your hand says and what Your silence shouts in the dark. I know how Your flesh cleaves and puckers when You bend Your body and how many little dimples form on Your breasts and how warm and deep Your breath comes out from inside You. I know everything, everything. How Your body falls on the bed with its lilylike paleness and nymphean charm. How You pucker Your lips and how the pupils of Your eyes wane in their pure white setting. And how Your right arm entwines itself wearily, snowy-white round my neck. I know what You want to say when You open Your mouth and I know what You see when You close Your eyes and what You are thinking when slowly and shyly Your cheeks turn red.

From the way You walk when You arrive and from the warmth of Your hand when You greet me I know how many kisses You will give me and what You will say to me. I have probed You completely, O Doomed One! with the microscope that my dissolute soul holds... and behold—behold the glut keeps rising together with love.

Noon. The embraces of the Mighty Lover descend ablaze from Ouranos[22] and motionless earth becomes a Mother.

The crops, goldenly subdued, bow their heads heavily as though they are thinking, as though they foresee the sickle. Beyond, the mountains hush. The vast earth stretches out to sleep and the birds grow quiet in the trees and the animals rest beneath their shades. And in the endless heat, in the stillness of all things and all living creatures, in the fiery kisses of the sun that cover and impregnate the earth, a strange and secret creaking can be heard. As if the earth is trembling. From pleasure perhaps, or perhaps from pain.

And suddenly the blazing and unforgettable noon of our happiness — when the Mighty Sun of love was burning upon our souls — cut across my mind and body O Chosen One, like a nostalgia, like a flame.

III

October 12

Spring has shed its petals and the summer of our love is spent and the willows droop down at the river and their weeping echoes in the forests. A foreboding weighs upon the trees. An autumn weighs upon my heart. And when Your memory treads upon my soul the rasping of some inconsolable dreams, bedded down there weeping, wail at its passing —like fallen leaves crying out in pain at being trampled in the earth.

October 20

Despairingly I weave my arms about You and look into Your eyes. So You have nothing more to give me?

October 21

Some night I'd like to drag You into the forests' darkest depths where we could be alone without the stars above us, and have You tell me all the obscene words You know. And have You squeeze all the slime from Your lips that Your memory has locked inside it and is mortified to remember. Words that raise shame to the cheeks and sully the ears and lay bare the mysteries of nakedness.

A mucky desire slithers inside me and seeks to learn all the lewd words that You know. I want to see Your bashful lips profane themselves of their own volition. Without a trace of blushing, without hesitation, with well-versed mouth, bold glance and brazen stance. Let all Your unclean thoughts and all the wanton undulations of Your figure rise palpable and lustful in shameless procession before the statue of Ashtoreth.[23] We will celebrate the Priapeia[24] of our love, O Doomed One. I shall be motionless before You, peering into Your eyes. You must hide nothing from me, nothing! And You must spit out all the obscene words You know at me. Maybe You will be able to make me feel some new and unknown pleasure! The pleasure of contempt and disgust and of love's desecration. I will clasp You then with an animal embrace in the orgasmic night. And I will feel something of my own sputtering in my hands, a creation of my pain — a body that I shaped and I corrupted — a fleshly organ of my ennui and of the deep incurable corruption of my mind. I will embrace You whole because You will be all mine and at last I will feel upon You the great triumph that great Conquerors and great Destroyers and Creators feel!

October 22

I am restless, restless. A pain has wakened in me. I am ill, my hands are burning. I feel that if I tear Your flesh a bit and see a bit — O just a drop! of blood, that I shall rest.

October 25

This morning I went down to my garden to breathe. The flowers were wide awake and, bowing with dewy weight, were saying their aromatic prayers to the morning star. A lone lily in the climbing vines was asleep. I could see a tiny lovely insect slowly coming out of its half-closed leaves — opening its wings with effort as if they were loaded down with pollen maybe, or perhaps with sensuality. It had spent the night inside the lily. I watched it flitting clumsily among the trees, drunk with pleasure. I sensed that its eyes were probably filled with the memory and desire of the night — and could not see. Somewhere out there in the trees the spider was spinning her web all night, waiting. O how it sputtered in the webbing of death! The spider pounced on the victim — and I passed wearily beneath the branches without a word, without lifting a hand to save the unfortunate victim of love!

I forgot it completely. It never crossed my mind all day. But at night, at daybreak, when I wearily emerged from her embrace, drunk from the kisses that her lips were treating me to all night — I don't know why, I suddenly remembered the hapless insect and I saw the spider hanging there somewhere, hanging the great web of death.

October 29

O there is so much I feel that others do not feel! I sit here now at midnight thinking. She has just left, tired but also sad because I sent her away. When I bent over her and rested my brow between her breasts and felt something like bliss and forgetfulness slipping inside me and calming my pain, an enormous rage shook me. It suddenly felt as though Someone from above had tossed me this mass of flesh and these eyes and red lips and softness of voice to lull me to sleep — like a toy they give to babies to keep them from crying. And something wells up inside me like defiance, like mockery, like a wave, and I feel the urge to stomp on this crumb they are tossing at me who is dying of hunger. No, no, it is something else that I seek, something else, something else . . .

And I drag myself to the window and watch the night mutely spreading out and enveloping me. The trees are asleep. Above them the moon stands vigil. I can hear the soft breathing of the roses in their sleep. I lower my night-embraced head and listen to the silence, and I think to myself. What, after all, is it that I seek?

November 10

I have grown weary. My feet are bloody from life's journey. The wings of my soul have been singed in the furnace of prurience.

I have grown weary. Droplets of blood mark my path on the earth. The kingdom of desire is endless, my Chosen One, and endless the footpath of lamentation. My soul saw much and was blinded. Blind, without a cane, stooped from the weight of my entire generation's sorrow, banished from my Country, a criminal before birth — I have dragged myself as far as Your knees.

O Antigone of my soul — scatter Your golden hair on my feet and wipe the blood from them.

Give me Your hand, O Daughter of my pain, and lead me who am blind.

November 11

The worm crawls on the rose of love. The whole world cannot comfort my thought. And the world is larger than

You. I feel a vast yearning in me for the tall mountains and the broad horizons and the free air above the clouds. An eagle lurks inside me and tears at my heart. And seeks its Country. My soul has grown weary of walking the earth and my heart has grown weary of weeping. And of hearing the world's weeping and the mute pain of the stars and the inconsolable roar of the sea. My body has grown weary and my brow has grown strong and I want to lie down at last on the great bed, fold my hands and wait. Who knows! The ocean at its depths is eternally still and quiet and dead. Perhaps that other ocean up above us where the stars travel and cruise may also have endless depths beyond it, motionless dead depths where Life and Pain have never traveled — eternally azure shrouds for the souls of the Select and Martyred.

November 12

There are times when I feel it is not my imagination that tells me the eyes of my soul are watching day and night. Rather, I feel it is a supreme effort of my mind to remember. I come from other worlds loaded down with memories and tears and untamed desires. All-virginal and untouched by the evils of this world, I feel a soul in me weeping day and night. Weeping for those mysterious grievances and the half-extinguished memories and strange shadows that crawl across the dark dungeons of my memory like slow-motion phantoms in longtrailing shrouds. My soul comes from better worlds and my nostalgia for the stars is incurable. And the joys of this world are small for me and glory is but a mockery of my desires and love is unable to satisfy my heart. A mere drizzle falling on the burning sands of the deserts. A sleepwalker of this world, I pass through with open eyes and do not see. I carry strange worlds inside me that I look at night and day. Great and beautiful worlds that unite with the ache that sits motionless upon my soul. I walk on the soil and see vast seas of harmony before me and ships gliding by and disappearing and stars rising like suns and smiling— bygone acquaintances and bygone castles of my soul.

My soul has strayed into the stars along its journey. And Your hand is weak and small, O Most Beloved, and Your eyes are shallow and Your soul is from other smaller worlds and You cannot show me the right road, and at night when we are alone You cannot lift me in Your white arms and bring me to my Country.

November 15

O the wretched fragrances that pile up in the soul and wait! O the mystical Altar Table that spires in the sanctuary of the mind, covered with purple. And the mysterious closed book with the seven seals that is lying on it, waiting.

The Altar Gate is open and the holy Chalice is empty, hopelessly waiting year after year for the body and blood. And I join my hands and wait. I've grown pale and the shudder of black forebodings drains my knees of their strength. My soul buckles under the pain. The yearning of a great Liturgy is weeping inconsolable inside me. All my body and all my thoughts and all the longings of my flesh are waiting for the Great Holy Communion. And day and night I gaze into the depths of my soul where the holy Chalice shines, empty and hopeless.

And I fear . . . I begin to understand . . . and I sit mute— Adam banished king, and I remember some other Country and I weep—I weep the hopeless bitter weeping of the orphaned and the exiled.

You bend over me and Your kisses suck all my body and all my joy and You drag the treasure of caresses that are hidden in Your hands all over me and weave Yourself round me like the lusty vine round the Cypress tree — and I, unmoving, feeling neither joy nor sorrow, lie still and ponder. I ponder over the sunsets that are always beautiful and always the same and have so much melancholy and so much blood-soaked pain in their death struggle. I ponder over the stars that spill out like the tears of some invisible weeping God. You kiss me and make love to me . . . And from a distance one by one I hear the sighs of the lilies that are shedding on the waters, and the reveries of the violets under the leaves, and the weeping of the roses that are wounded by the thorns in the night. . . . A strange blooming of sensations opens in my soul and I hear the deep and boundless weeping of matter. . . . You bend over me, O Doomed One! and You kiss me and embrace me. And I feel neither joy nor sorrow. I do not see You. I, just another piece of weeping matter, stoop and ponder. . . . My soul is the aeolian lyre[25] caressed by the sigh of an entire world. All the sunsets' secrets weep in my eyes. And all the yearnings of the lofty-browed . . . You bend over me, O Doomed One, and kiss me and laugh ʻand sing of love and joy and life . . . And I sense You like an enormous lily bending over me lamenting — a doomed lily wounded by the roses' thorns . . .

November 18, Midnight

I feel entire worlds blooming inside me, monstrous and ghostly worlds. And all the blooms of my soul are huge satanic fully opened chrysanthemums that look like some prodigious artist's red and yellow brushstrokes. I am created for other worlds. I sense the profundity that the chosen souls of martyrs sense — the ocean and the flood and the enigma in the eyes of the great and the mysteries that are hidden deep in the creases of the lofty brows. Deep inside me the Nostalgia of another more beautiful Country holds sway and weeps.

November 20

I sense that the thing I am seeking is higher than love and higher than the joy of life and higher than science and glory and higher even than the stars. Don't keep my wings tied in Your embrace.

You are only a shadow and only a smile in the great journey of my soul. Your eyes are the two clear springs where my thoughts came to drink and rest for a moment. And between Your breasts hides the soft pillow where I slept for a moment in order to waken again. Don't hold me bound. The enigma is not hidden in Your Loins nor in Your enormous eyes. And Your arms are small and weak and do not embrace my entire soul. There is a magnet above the stars that pulls me. And my entire body shudders, magnetized by the Great Nostalgia and the Great Longing. Someone is pulling at me from the stars. Do not hold me bound. The thing I am seeking is higher than love and higher than the joy of life.

IV

November 28

I fell on the bed exhausted from the life of a whole day. Dense night was lying in wait outside my window and softly, blackly, spilled all about as I put out the light. I stretched my weary body across the bed, sank my head in the soft pillow and blissfully, deliciously, closed my eyes.

Peace and Serenity flowed sweetly over my body — something like luxuriant sensuality uncoiled inside me. Blissful, I closed my eyes. And I thought of the Great Night of Death.

December 6

A sunset without end is spreading inside me. A sun in me is dying. And a red shroud is dragging itself to shreds upon the waters. Everything in my heart is hushing into that heavy stillness that covers great struggles and great corpses.

And a bell's funereal echoes are tolling in my soul — and I understand, it's like the bell in the wind at night that is quietly weeping for the day that is dying.

December 11

Some secret body has collapsed in my heart and is dying. Something gigantic in my heart is gasping its last breath.

December 15

At times I feel the urge to do a painting of my soul. In that eternal grouping of Laocoön.²⁶ The serpents of Knowledge and the spasms of Pain. And the silent and unending strangling of my dream children.

December 22

I feel an enormous "Tower of Hunger" inside me, inside my heart. Someone has locked me in there together with my dreams. I heard the door being nailed shut and the keys being tossed in the river. I look my dreams in the eye and fall silent. The tears have dried and I am mute and still and the days pass over the skylight and my children weep and circle about me. One by one each falls on its face at my feet, dead. And I am left alone. Their corpses, lovely and pale, pile around me wide eyed as though still complaining. And I am blind and look for them in the night of my heart... In the night of my heart a father weeps and looks for his children.

December 22, Daybreak

In Rama was there a voice heard, mourning and weeping and great lamentation. Rachel was weeping for her children and would not be comforted because they are not.

I could not sleep. A nightmare—a thought—was pressing on my breast and I had to go out to breathe. I wanted to run, to run until I tired my body and blistered my feet and grew exhausted—to forget. So that I would no longer see those eyes that have so much innocence and virginity and so much blue happiness in their depths. Eyes that hide an entire world asleep in their depths and complain to me, without their knowing it. And I walk the deserted streets at night out under the trees, and ponder. And I see things others do not see. And I walk and understand. A microscope is stationed before the eyes of my soul and poisons my life. The others have eyes that are bare and they do not see the mysteries. When I stoop over gurgling clear-flowing water and get close to quench my thirst—the microscope shows me clusters of worms and myriad microbes and tiny monsters that are swimming and playing and kissing and spreading their tentacles and lying in ambush. When I get close to the rose to smell it I see its ugly naked fibers inside the leaves, and I see a thousand living things crawling on it and slimy organisms chasing each other.

I see the lips of beautiful women crawling with sinful indecent kisses. I discern the wrinkles on their foreheads and the nights' passions and vulgar loves in the dark refuge of their eyes. And when I abandon myself to pleasure I see the darkening shadow of remorse and boundless pain approaching to begin their conquering. I see black-winged night falling in a heap behind Your eyes, O Doomed One. And in the carnal pleasure that paralyzes and enervates our bodies and in the echo of our kisses and in the erotic hollow of our bed that knows so many of our secrets—the microscope unmoving before the eyes of my soul reveals to me two horrible skeletons embracing, and I hear the creaking of their bones, and deep, deep in my soul I hear the chill and horror of the tombs.

O when I imagine You in the tomb, wild instincts of sensuality and horror rise like waves in my blood and I feel the urge to grab You and press my lips on Your lips and clasp You with all the strength of hopelessness and love, to become one flesh, to melt together in the same flame of one embrace — to compress our whole body in one unending kiss and die at night, at midnight, in a single thunderbolt of pleasure — so that death will find nothing to take but a few ashes.

Give me Your lips and give me Your flesh, all of it, and all the charm of Your movements and every undulation of Your body. Here beneath the stars tonight wild prurient passions are rising in my blood, and wild shivers of death. I am going to embrace You whole tonight and knead You all over in my hands, and leave the burning marks of my incurable passion on Your body. Don't You, too, sense it, here beneath the moon that drags its incurable pain across the heavens like an enormous funeral urn, don't You sense the urgency to hasten to enjoy, and don't You hear rising round us, moaning and encircling us ever more closely, ever more closely, the great the mute sea of Death?

Something is straining in my mind. Something wild like madness and like love is running riot in my soul. I am afraid of going mad! My eyes see deep, so very deep, and weep.

Come, as long as we are going to die, as long as the skeletons are bedded inconsolable down in the soil, let us make haste. Come, everything is dying around us. The flowers are dying and wilting beneath us, and O all the stars that are dying above us! How many luminous inconsolable dramas are roving up there over our heads—in the eternal horror and the eternal silence!

Come, give me Your lips and do not deny me Your flesh. I want to weave my body around Yours and drain the treasure in my lips upon You, O Doomed One, and poison Your soul with the poison of my forebodings.

December 27

The cataclysm was covering the world. Two hands belonging to a doomed mother who was drowning could still be seen outside the waters desperately holding up an infant to be saved.

And the cataclysm keeps rising, rising . . .

December 31

Roses, roses, roses, that I may decorate my soul before it dies. And may the night be moonless and may we both be there with heavy mute desire passing over us. And may the final flash of our love be like a conflagration and may the dead of night turn red with shame and may our lips stay fixed in one unending mute, immobile kiss. And may the cantharis of our kiss race through the deep night and waken the loins of all the animals in the depths of the forests and drive them mad with the orgasm of nighttime coupling, and may it pass over the flowers and loosen their girdles and reveal all their secrets . . .

Roses, roses, roses, that I may decorate my soul before it dies. A vast ache is rising in my heart and I want to clasp

You tightly, O Doomed One, O Loved One! with all the strength of my body—like the animals that wrestle at night in the forests when the heat of desire burns and beats at their loins.

A vast ache is rising in my heart and the flames of voluptuousness and orgiastic revelry ignite in my eyes and laughter trembles and writhes with pain on my lips. My soul resembles those who have gone mad with grief and break out laughing.

Roses, roses, roses. As long as I cannot cry I may as well begin to laugh. My laughter is a convulsion and my love, O Doomed One, is like madness and like hatred and like contempt. And my kisses are like bites. I pause and look into Your eyes and clasp You in my arms and gaze at You. And I don't know if I hate You and want to strangle You or if I'm crazed with love and want us both to be united, socket interlocked with socket, in a motionless embrace throughout the nights.

January 2

No, my Beloved, don't cry. Your tears drip on me and burn all my flesh and all my soul. Don't cry my Beloved. It's not Your fault if Your heart doesn't comfort my brow. It's not Your fault if the lullaby of Your kisses round my lips each night can't lull my pain to sleep. It's the pain of love that has conquered me completely. It's the eternal disillusionment that follows happy longing. O poor closed flower petals that hide the nakedness, and the sun's licentious hand that opens them to savor them and promptly wither them! O the eternal brutality and desecration of love! We profaned our thoughts, O Shunammite[27] of my soul, in the mystic temples of Phoenicia's rays and in the occult groves where instincts revel and priestesses lie in wait and the flesh of Astarte rears omnipotent and indomitable. My soul has grown weary and a quiver of disgust and contempt pushes upward from the chasteness that still remains to it.

O the disgust of kisses and fecund loins!

The wooden statue of the goddess of Fertility came to the sandy shores of Greece one day from the mysterious altars of Chaldaea and from the licentious shrines of Syria, a joyless brazen statue with a stupid smile on its thick lips. And from there one day — ravishingly beautiful, proud and modest about her nakedness, with her hand over her breasts to hide them and at her loins to keep them from showing, white and virginal and Hellenic — sprang the Goddess of Beauty. . . . O my Beloved, the nostalgia for chasteness rises in me. I, Praxiteles of love, want to erect the statue of the Heavenly Aphrodite in the debris of the Pandemos. O Beloved! a white longing is mowing down the roses and ivy inside me, and my soul is trembling for the great sowing of the lilies.

January 3

Oh! the song has departed and returns no more from the stars. The girdle has fallen from the flower and the fragrance has spilled and the whiteness has been profaned. The caterpillar of desire has sullied the petals. The bitterness of kisses clings to my lips and a nausea is rising in me — the great, the terrible nausea of love. Don't weave Your caresses round my neck and don't cry. Don't condescend to cry. Let the sea of Destiny keep rising round us and let the mighty Curse keep spreading over our heads. Don't cry. A stepmother is hovering over our lives — like a falcon over turtle doves — envious and harsh. How many times did I kiss You and how many times did You writhe with pleasure on the sheets? You don't remember. You don't remember but She does. They were recorded and weighed up there, O Doomed One, by the Great Power that is eternally envious and eternally taking revenge. You don't remember, but She does. So now don't cry. Come, bind yourself tightly round us, O Doomed Ivy, the sea that circles me keeps rising, rising. No, neither prayer nor supplication will blemish my lips. Pain has strengthened and rendered my soul proud, and it breaks but does not bend. I will die unmoving, silent, without a spasm, without entreaty. And I will die happy because I will drag You with me — I will drag You with me to the grave, O Doomed One, O Beloved.

January 5

I made her shudder with horror tonight. She had crept to my lips, lovely and thirsty. Like a nightingale creeping toward the eyes of the serpent. I was anxious to see how she would react to the surprise I had prepared for her. I led her, laughing and wordless to the bed. It was dark now and the windows were closed. Outside the whistling of the wind could be heard through the trees. The moaning of the sea was coming from a distance like a sigh out of an enormous breast. I had put out the lamp and only a small candle was fending off the darkness surrounding us. I led her, laughing and wordless, to the bed and covered her eyes with my lips. A horror was suspended above us. And when she opened her eyes and saw what was over the bed, O poor thing! a cry of terror tore from her breast, her eyes flew open and froze with fear as they stared up at it. Her body shook all over. Gleaming on a piece of black velvet up there was a stark white skull that I had hung as an ornament. Its jaws were open as though it were laughing. And in the corners of its eyes certain black mysteries were sleeping.

I can still feel the shuddering of Your body in my arms, O Doomed One! She slid down from the bed and hid her face in her trembling hands. Big silent tears flowed from her eyes. A horrible spasm was moving her upper lip and her whole body was trembling. This is how cane sways under the cold breath of night. I was looking into her eyes, watching the entire evolution of fear. And when I stooped to kiss her in order to quiet her, she fell in a heap at my feet and clasped my knees and entreated me.

This—I thought—is how they used to entreat the Gods.

She entreated me to have pity on her and to love her only and not torment her. What did she do to me that I should torment her? What did I ask of her that she did not give me? And she cried and entreated. Despairing. The tops of the trees outside were swaying and the leaves were calling out. I could feel the hapless roses, poor things, that are unable to resist and fight—the hapless roses were shedding their petals out in the garden...

January 6

You don't understand me. You still have not understood me. There is joy in the night of the tombs and myriad night-ingales sing in the cypress trees. And the laughter of the skulls is true and guileless. Last night as I was watching You entreating me an unspeakable pain was mowing down the hopes inside me. You do not understand me.

The skull of the dead is the most beautiful symbol of Love, and the most lascivious ornament for beds. Does it not generate wild desires in You to embrace and kiss before You die? And don't You feel how many desires and how much cantharis drip from its mute eyes and the fleshless space between the lips and spread themselves across the sheets?

You don't understand me my Love, I haven't poisoned

You completely yet. When You understand the meaning of the seashore's sigh, and what the caves at night are saying, and what the stars are echoing up there and why they are trembling. When You can hear the weeping of flowers and souls as they are being born, when You can tell me why the jaws beneath the earth are laughing, and what things shudder and weep in the air—then I will clasp You whole in my embrace and kiss You whole, because You will then be wholly mine—both body and soul.

When You come one night smiling and happy and press me tightly to Your breasts and tell me: Come, Beloved, the Desire of Death is rising in me... the sweetness of the eternal kiss is racing in me and entreating me—then I will embrace You whole because You will be wholly mine.

January 7

I am afraid I shall go mad. Strange creakings resonate inside me, secret chords are breaking in my heart, huge tears are dripping and pitting my brain. I feel things that others do not feel. When I go out to my garden at night I know what the roses are saying and what the jasmine reply, and what shy things the violets are thinking and dreaming. I know what the leaden colors of the clouds are saying and what painful secrets the squawking ravens passing over me have seen. And when I walk I shudder all over because I feel worlds being destroyed under my every step, and ants gasping their last breath and insects dying. The stars up there are writing letters of another world's language and I read them and turn pale. And when she is coming I can sense it no matter how far away she is, and I tremble all over like a needle being approached by a magnet. I am afraid I shall go mad. Thoughts are being born inside me that blaze without shedding light, and that leave tracks without passing. Wild crazy songs burst out of me that burn my lips. The desires of my soul have bolted, they are hurtling me toward the chasm, I can sense it. It doesn't matter. Landscapes are changing. I fold my hands and allow myself to keep running, and running.

Past vast, still seas, or towering trees that thunderbolts keep felling into heaps, or next to green verdant plains with huge exotic splotches of blood—like poppies. Or alongside beds of flowers, mysteriously plaited, that smile and lurk in the dark bowers. I perceive everything, everything. From the lightest murmur of kisses that echoes in the nests at night, or from the sighing of the lilies under the moon—to the boundless harmony that controls the stars. I see the mysteries that the select see. And I have grown pale and my soul has fallen ill and is withering from the holy thirst of death.

January 10

O, if only it were fated that I could elevate my mind to my desires and one day invite all mankind before me, and teach what I perceive.

January 10, Midnight

There are times, I don't know why, when I perceive more clearly that we are the buffoons of invisible powers. Play-actors, playing out the comedy of life, and entertaining them. And I perceive it is time to break our bonds and tear down the curtain and preach suffering and the curse and the great anathema. Joy and love and faith, nighttime fan-

tasies of the mind, were wiped out in the first bloody smile of
dawn. And nothing more remains for us except the weariness and curse and exhaustion of the mind and the pain of
Truth. The eagle of Prometheus has not died because it is
eternal, but the smile that blooms on all the marble statues
and in the lives of our simple forebears has today been
reduced to the horrible enigma of jaws in Hamletian skulls.
We live, we struggle, we embrace, we hate—wretched creatures—and suddenly the earth opens under our feet and we
fall one on top of the other, mute, yellow, and despairing.
Not a hope. The grave is eternal night—the eternal rotting
of bones, hopes, thoughts. O the anguished anger that rises
like a curse, like a brokenhearted sob, like a flood! O the
great countenances that die, and the great lovely eyes that
close!...

January 12

No! You will never feel the disgust that I feel. The great
nausea that I feel for the masses. A proud Tower rises like
an Acropolis in my soul. There is not a single footpath leading to the Tower, not a single bridge unites it with the
world. It is isolated and unapproachable, without windows
and without doors. Below, my other soul spreads out with a
thousand roads that are free and open wide to the masses.
Thousands walk there, coming and going and soiling the
lower parts of my soul. Not a single path leads up to the
Tower. The masses will never be able to climb to the Tower.

And I come and go in the Tower, speechless, without joy
and without pain, indifferent to all, alone and solitary. Its
rooms are large and cold and uninhabited. Below in my soul
I hear the masses shouting and finding fault and ridiculing.
Their shouts and reproaches and laughter reach my Tower
like the droning of insects. And I feel a deep contempt for

those parts of my soul that have contact with the world. And my ego spreads out like a sea inside me and a smile of joy rises in my mind: Vulgar contact with the rabble is never going to contaminate my Tower and its marble floor is never going to be soiled by the mud of their footsteps, and their hands and eyes and thoughts will never pollute the Holy of Holies of my soul.

January 15

What are those clouds that rise above the sea one after the other and settle in my heart?

January 16

I feel as though someone is in the air watching me. A huge eye that doesn't know sleep, that doesn't know tears. It looks deep, deep into my soul. And I seem to be following it. Wherever I go it drags me magnetized behind it, lifeless, without will and with inconsolable desires. It looks at me and I feel it as it penetrates inside me and tears away at something and looks at what is happening in my soul, and keeps silent and shows no mercy. And I understand, I am a puppet that a hand has lifted up on the cosmic stage so that I could amuse some unknown powers — I am a vassal of the hand that pushes me, a slavish echo of an omnipotent voice. I feel as though someone is in the air watching me. And an anguished rage bursts in me and I don't want to become a plaything of the unknown Powers and I will no longer allow my soul to be the laughingstock of the merciless Eye. It follows me as if I am some sort of drama — I can see it sitting up there in the gallery watching. Yesterday I fled into a dense thicket in the depths of the forest. I feel I shall go mad. Sweat was pouring out of me. I was uneasy. How can it follow me here, I kept telling myself, how can it get into the foliage and hoe my soul? But still I sensed something. I sensed something crawling slowly and patiently with measured movements over my forehead. It was It. And I shuddered. I raised my head. The Eye was motionless and watching me. And now I could discern some kind of joy in its depths. O horror! how well I was playing my part!

January 20

No, I can no longer suffer this. My body is tired and I want to lie down. To close my eyes and rest. Something has been dying inside me throughout the day, some fiber is breaking. It has furrowed and plowed my forehead with its gaze. At night when I lie down to sleep, at first a kind of darkness starts to spread before me. And I feel it lurking in there somewhere. And I tremble. I pull the covers over my head and hide my face. And I see. Darkness facing me, vast as a sea. Everything hushes as though in expectation of Someone. And slowly, slowly in the darkness a sun rises — a strange sun, without rays, without warmth — a steely, luminous, ghastly disc. The Eye. I tremble. Terror stricken I waken and there on the white canopy of the bed in its assigned place watching me motionless, sits the Eye.

January 21

Don't tremble my Love. I am Your Beloved. Don't be afraid of the dark. We will shut ourselves in here together.

No one will be able to enter. I will light the small lamp with the crimson shade to give a rosy glow to the sheets because their whiteness startles me. So shroudlike are they.

And when the doomed girl stretched her body on the sheets that were like shrouds, and when she wound her arms about my neck and wound her body round my body, and when she gave me her lips and I bent over her eyes—I smiled.

O! when I realize that I can die whenever I wish, a wild joy floods my ego, I feel an omnipotence in my hands—and I smile.

I embrace You now with confidence and redoubled love. The undulation of Your body will never slip away from my embrace. You will remain faithful to me eternally. We shall embrace, the two of us, indifferent to all else, we shall hear nothing, the centuries will pass over us in vain, so will men's enmities and the roar of life. The embrace will be ghastly down there, I know, but it will be eternal. And you will be near me always and will never leave, and when all the corpses rise at midnight You will not be able to rise because Your limbs will be joined with my limbs and no one will perceive the love and horror being celebrated down there.

January 23

Endless sea. Tranquil and deep, without a single wave. Or a glimpse of seashore. The sky, heavy and cloudy. Not a seagull in the air, nor a fish in the moribund waters.

Only in the middle, in the middle of the sea a boat with a curious shape—like a coffin—is advancing on the waters, without a sail, without oars and without a rudder; slowly, slowly it advances on the waters, and the water barely shows around the prow that it silently cuts through it. As though

79

an invisible hand from above were pushing it. And, O my Love, I felt as though the two of us were in the boat, lying side by side, with a waxen cross in our mouths—side by side, dead.

January 25

A world has collapsed inside me. Now and then when my soul is still transparent I bend over it and look at the secrets in its depths. The great white marbles are broken and piled in a heap beneath the domes of their ruined temples. The columns of the royal palaces have tilted and cracked, and the waters are seeping in and eroding and peeling away the great, the magnificent paintings. The bells no longer toll. The gardens within are withering and birds are no longer on the branches singing. A few poor little houses have remained. Some marble columns are still standing. And every day a knock and a threnodial sound echoes in my heart and I say to myself, unmoving, calm, and hopeless: Some marble column is falling.

January 26, Midnight

I sit here thinking about the doomed birds that creep bewitched toward the serpent's eyes. It fixes its eyes on the bird and the bird at once begins to tremble as if seized by convulsions. A cry of agony and terror escapes from its throat and the passing wayfarer instantly senses that a serpent is nearby. The poor bird races up and down the branch seemingly trying to escape. But it keeps drawing closer. The serpent coiled around the tree trunk has its eyes fixed motionless. And the bird keeps drawing closer and closer and finally falls headlong into the serpent's open mouth.

I sit and think and weep over the things that drag themselves bewitched and despairing toward Death.

February 20

"Give me Your eyes that I may close them with my lips to keep them from looking upward. Let me place my hand on Your brow to cool Your thought. Come, lean on me; It is I who desire Your kisses and it is I who desire Your love, O my Lover! Come to me again as You did before, that we may run together hand in hand on the violet strewn paths of our love. Come, my lips are thirsty, the night is lovely, the moon more silvery, the stars more enamored. Come, I am Your Beloved. We will go to the edge of the seashore, we will sit on a reef and, cradled in Your arms, I will listen to the harmony of the murmur of the sea coupled with the hymn of our kisses. And slowly you'll embrace my body, and plunge Your eyes deep into mine, and bit by bit spill all Your love into my lips."

I feel a God inside me shooting darts at my dreams. I feel blood flowing like a river inside me. And the sound of strange wounded sighs in my soul.

Rest Your cheek on mine, try to hold back Your trears, don't let Your heart break under the pain, and listen: I am going to spill all my love bit by bit into Your lips.

I know an island that rises out there, You don't see it, but I do — out there where the sky kisses the sea. It is from there that they embark and cross the waters and come and find me — those endless notes of lovers' songs that toll at midnight and walk across the waves and reach my heart. I feel them entering inside me, pleading.

They tightly weave themselves about my soul and serenade it with strange, O such strange words, and pull it to that panharmonious island way out there. White arms are emerging out there in the waves, do You see them? they are beckoning me to go, and great lovely eyes are looking at me invitingly . . . Don't cry my Beloved, don't. Hold back Your pain and listen to all my love. Don't say that I am mad. You do not see, but I do.

A boat has left the island and is slowly gliding toward us on the sea, to take us. Come, my Beloved, we will lie on the boat, love's desire will swell the sails, the great Tranquillity will stretch out over the waves, I will weave my arm about Your neck, I will ask for Your lips and we will fall asleep. The roar of life out there along the seashore will no longer interrupt our embraces. Vulgar contact with the world will no longer contaminate our love. We will be alone on the sea, plunged in the panharmonious song that will be emerging from the enchanted island and the white arms will be pushing the boat and the lovely large eyes will be ahead leading the way. And we will lock the ages in our hearts. And time will stand still and will no longer soil our love. And the stars will be rolling over us, and worlds will be dying, and misery will be reigning and killing, and we will be still, in love, and our sea will be tranquil and our sails full and the large eyes ahead will glow like the moon and our boat will be pulling eternally toward the mystery and the harmony.

March 2

I am at peace.
I am at peace because I am without hope.

I am at peace, at peace — a shroud has draped itself over my soul, an invisible hand is pushing me and the heavy voice of someone else speaks and commands inside me. Someone spoke inside me and I obeyed. And I ran to my house in the country far from men. And I wrote her to come here where our love will be great and tranquil like the surrounding mountains.

I am at peace, completely at peace. She replied joyfully that she will come. She hopes my love will be restored to health here in the mountains and verdure, and that my lips will no longer utter blasphemies, but will kiss only. She will come joyfully.

I am alone. I brought all my paintings and have hung them on the walls. The chrysanthemums and the outlandish designs and the suns that are setting.

I am at peace, completely at peace. And the voice was heard in my soul and I obeyed. And I ran quickly — a hand pushed me. I understood; it was the same hand that had pushed me when I first saw her. And I ran down to the garden and cut as many flowers as I could find. The bed was buried under the lilies and roses. The floor beneath overflowed with them. I sent for more flowers. A heavy fragrance scatters and presses on my breast — like aromatic death. I close the windows and doors.

I am at peace. Completely at peace. A strange joy rises and falls in my breast. Like a sob. And yet I feel it is a joy — maybe it is so very great that it tears through my throat. She will come, I'll have the windows shut, she will be startled by the fragrance, I'll quickly close the door and kneel before her and ask for her lips. O I'm not mad! I'm not mad! I will coil myself around her and ask her for the eternal kiss . . . O Doomed One! . . . I feel I would not be able to resist Your pain if the sweetness of Death were not spilling sovereignlike in my soul. O the Great Journey! I feel a mad joy surging in me, weeping. I have shut all the windows and doors. If the fragrance of the flowers cannot bring us to eternal peace—I have with me, as a last resort, a precious poison that brings eternal joy, the Great Joy, without pain.

I am at peace, completely at peace. I sit in the defoliated garden and ponder. I look across the white path where She will appear, laughing, with that lissome body and those tranquil eyes that are probably now mirroring the green calm of the fields.

In the night, the path that is going to bring her resembles a running winding serpent that has stopped in front of me.

And I ponder. At times in my sleep I see a ghastly dream, and a strange consolation comes over me, and I reason: It's a dream... If I wish, with one abrupt movement of my body I can waken and escape. And I ponder. Could it be tht all this life of mine has been a strange dream, could it be that all this love and all the horror and hope of death are things I see in a great sleep and finally, tonight, now that I am sitting in this defoliated garden waiting for Her, I have decided with one abrupt movement of my body to waken and escape from the dream? I ponder: is the dream just starting, or is it just ending? O, how something aches inside me! How I ache in my heart! Despairing thoughts tear my mind like lightening streaks and in their glow I manage to discern memories of other worlds, distant, distant memories of sunken Atlantises!...

The tranquil, endless sea spreads out before me. Violets are silently descending from the sky and spilling into the west. The star of love is smiling on the waters. I feel we are alone, my Love, in a tiny boat with jet black sails, like the wings of a raven. Rowing mournfully, mournfully toward an unknown destination. We do not speak because a deep sob is rising and constricting our throats. And we row forever mournful on the waters toward an unknown destination, toward the west, our eyes focused out there on the gold and bloodied clouds where the sun is lingeringly dying.

I sit and ponder in the defoliated garden. Night is beginning to spill over the trees. The stars are preparing to open in the heavens. Joy-turned-sorrow now is stopped in my throat. The sea from a distance is singing the voluptuousness of death. A mysterious flame is pulling the stars in the heavens. Serenity is spreading over all the peaks, and the leaves are talking ever so softly on the trees...

O Doomed One! Doomed One! I feel the urge to flee and hide in the depths of the forest and lie on the ground and let my tears flow, let them flow for You, whom Fate decreed should know me!...

Here ended the diary of the heart of my unfortunate friend—the prodigious artist—written helter skelter on loose pages in a nervous erratic handwriting.

The servant came one morning, frightened, and called me to hurry to my friend's villa. I suspected some disaster as I knew my friend and his love. We broke down the door to the room and a suffocating odor of flowers overwhelmed us. I quickly opened the windows and doors.

Dreadful sight! She had dragged herself as far as the window, apparently to open it. The flowers at her feet beneath the window were trampled and crushed, her fingers bloodied —everything indicated that she had struggled desperately, poor thing, to open the window to breathe—but he did not let her.

And she had fallen, pale and exhausted, her eyes wide open with terror. A spasm of horror and fright—and hatred —distorted her lovely innocent face. Her lissome body had dropped despairing and dead on the flowers. And he, with a tranquil smile, had stretched out at her side and thrown his arms around her neck in an inexpressible gesture of love.

Above them hung a curious picture that showed the doleful course the hapless brilliant artist's reason had taken lately.

An enormous serpent was uncoiling and running across the sand of a vast desert where a flame-red sun was setting, bloodying the sky. And in its mouth that dripped poison it was holding and caressing and biting a tiny stark-white wilted lily.

The Sickness of the Age

The Sickness of the Age*

If we go back to the childhood years of man we find no trace of this sickness. The first people were simple, their hearts were guileless and serene, their souls were sketched in large outlines. Nature unfolded like a miracle and a smile before them. Everything was virginal and alive to them. The art of reasoning had not yet developed and did not poison all the joys and could not find the nullity and pain beneath the dazzling appearance. Inner man had not yet been touched by subtle psychological observations, by analysis and science.

The soul opened gradually, and viewed the world in astonishment, and smiled. A simple patriarchal people trickled down into the plains from the lofty plateaus of Tibet, with their huts along the shores of the lakes, their caves at the foot of the mountains, their transient tents on the desert sands.

Their sentiments were simple and expansive and wild. Love was artless, primitive—still an instinct.

Everything was ingenuous then. God would come down to the mountaintops. Manna would fall from heaven, and springs would gush out of the rocks. Gods would descend to earth and unite with the daughters of men. Men would ascend to heaven and unite with goddesses. Heaven communicated with earth via the magical ladder of simplicity. Indeed, they were so close in those days that the cows would raise their heads and lick the heavens with their tongues.

*This essay, under the pseudonym Karma Nirvami, is the first of N. Kazantzakis's works to appear in print after *Serpent and Lily*.

The mighty sun that scorches, dazzles, and blinds had not yet risen.

A certain light smiled on all their marble works and all their thoughts. A certain candor that we prudes and hypocrites do not know. Behold the Parthenon. It is light and honesty. Read the Mahabharata of the Hindus. The lover "drinks" the lips of his beloved all night, and somewhere it says the embrace is so savage that "the woman's breasts sink into the man's and the ornaments and necklaces that fill every bare spot on her body burst." This, then, is the love of early man. Read the *Song of Songs* to the beautiful Shunammite. Love was not a sin then and had the right to be honest. Sappho—the first liberated woman in history—sighed at night because she was alone and she did not hesitate to say it:

> The moon has set
> the Pleiades too; 'tis midnight
> the hours pass
> and I lie alone.

And, overcome with love, she flings away the shuttle of her loom and says to her mother:

> I cannot weave at my loom, o Mother.
> Night's Aphrodite o'erpowers me with desire for a youth.

Such guilelessness, such frankness, such joy and complete understanding of life! All the good things are here in this world. Beyond, nothing but ghosts and dead idols in meadows of daffodils. Achilles would have been glad to exchange his place as chief in Hades for that of slave on earth. It was enough for him just to see "the dazzling light of the sun."

The ancients combined perfectly the demands of the body and the demands of the soul. Never has a more perfect balance been revealed in history. From the gymnasium, to the Academy of Plato; from Knossos, Socrates gradually makes his way to Mount Ida, teaching and receiving inspiration for the Laws.[1]

Plato's *Symposium,* it seems to me, is a miniature of the Hellenic world. I never tire of reading it . . . Socrates and Aristophanes and Phaedrus and the others reclining on the double couches around the table. Wreaths of roses and violets on their heads. Handsome youths pouring drinks from a beautiful krater.[2] Discoursing and drinking, slowly and grandly rising to the loftiest peaks of Idealism. Crowned in roses and violets they philosophize, and on the lips of Socrates the words of Diotima take on the most divine flight that the human mind has ever known. And the doors fling open and in bursts Alcibiades, the handsomest Hellene, with ivy in his black hair and lovely flute girls in his company embracing him. And the wine flows more abundantly and old Socrates smiles and rearranges himself on the couch to make room for Alcibiades to stretch out.

I never tire of reading Plato's *Symposium.* It is for me the great, the holy revelation of the Hellenic world. I see that whole sunken Atlantis rising from the waves of bygone years the way—remember?—the way Phryne rose one day out of the Saronic waves, lovely and naked before all the Hellenes —the most modest and most beautiful of all the *hetairai*![3]

The religion of the Beautiful reigned then. Apollo—the handsome Muse Chief—was the personification of the Hellenic soul. In Sicily the city of Segesta erected a temple to its most beautiful citizen. Contests were held for the most handsome among adult males, among elders, and among boys. In Megara they held kissing contests among adolescents where, as Theokritos says, *"he who most sweetly joins his lips with another, crown-laden returns to his mother."*

This is what the Greek world was like. Melancholy was

unknown. The great problems had not yet distorted the soul with Pain. Look at how all their temples and all their statues and all their thoughts smile!...

Like all beautiful things—the Greek world, too, died quickly. It died in the superhuman and inhuman dispassion of the Stoics, in the various schools* of hysteria and despair, in the debauchery of the derailed followers of Epicurus.

Apollo, the beautiful God, the smile of Olympos, died. And from the east appeared the Son of the Virgin—the father of today's sickness of the soul.

Until the time of Jesus, man honored life and the good things of this world. He wanted to be beautiful and healthy and young and rich. He wanted to enjoy life and he knew how to enjoy it.

Jesus appeared—a pale visionary, reared in the torrid suns of Palestine, in the still and placid dreaminess of Lake Gennesaret.

He went up to the mount one day, gentle and serene and beautiful, and mankind followed him. "Blessed are the poor in spirit," he said with a smile. "Blessed are the hungry and thirsty. Blessed are the mourners."

The pale Nazarene climbed to the Parthenon and drove away the Mighty Gods Apollo and Artemis, and the smile of Aphrodite, and the cheer of Dionysos—"and extinguished the inextinguishable smile of the Gods."

And hagiographics and crosses spread over the marble: silent Madonnas with downcast eyes, pale weeping Madonnas, saints in martyrdom, sick and bloody flesh.

A heavy odor of incense spread over the world. And the roses withered, and the rosemary and palm tree, and the cypress and willow tree grew strong.

He brought love and goodness and humility into the world. Yes. But also the incurable Pain and the great Nos-

*τῶν Πεισιθανάτων, τῶν Ηγησιακῶν, καὶ τῶν Ἀννικερίων.

talgia and the eternal preoccupation with a world *where there is no anguish,* beautiful and blessed . . . but non-existent!

Love thine enemies. Come unto me all ye that are heavy laden and I will give ye rest. Father, forgive them for they know not what they do. Where did these strange, these first-heard words come from? What tranquil world could those large, those azure eyes have conceivably been turned toward?

It doesn't matter. Mankind heard and was seduced.

From that hour, neither joy nor pleasure!

It was a time of hair shirts on the flesh, ashes on the fore-head, genuflections, incessant crossings, and the harsh suppression of nature out there in the cloisters of the Lybian sands, in the vast towering silent monasteries.

The beautiful was a sin, and joy was nothing more, then, but prayer. All those queues of virgins with pale, unkissed lips pass before the eyes of my soul . . . Virgins who died without enjoying the great shudder of life; bodies barren and white—flowers that withered under the shade of the cross . . .

What epic dramas those ruined walls of the great monasteries could reveal to us, and what despair those grass-covered stones in the cemeteries must cover!

The riches of this world were scorned. Eyes were turned upward toward Higher Jerusalem, the Eternal Chimera, the Kingdom of Heaven, where we would be seeing God face to face from morning to night! And you die. And the soil is thrown over you and you wait. With hands crossed, a wax cross in your mouth, you lie there, waiting. The trumpet of resurrection does not sound. The angels are long in appearing. And you wait. In the meantime you rot and return to Mother earth and are transformed into the great, the horrible, the desperate metamorphosis of organic matter. And you spill without EGO into the soil as fertilizer, and the flowers that are nourished from your body revel about you. And men become dreamers and grow sensitive. The soul withdraws into mystic and religious ecstasies. Saint Theresa loves Christ in the flesh. And how many monks in those half-lit silent churches had not themselves been enamored of the pale Madonnas!

Sensitivity, ecstasy, reverie, are sentiments unknown to the ancient world, that sober and measured world that knew what it wanted and how to want, and that knew the inestimable value of this world's attractions.

The Barbarians from the North pour into civilized Europe and destroy the monuments of art, raising ignorance to the throne. And the former conquerers come dragging in defeat to the monasteries, grieving their loss. There is a need —unknown in antiquity—for them to pour their sentiments out to someone else. They have need of something to lean on, of a heart to feel for them. Unable to walk through life alone, lacking courage, their soul seeks a companion, a friend, man or woman, and gradually a new sentiment is born—Eros.

Eros as they understood it then and essentially as we understand it still today.

Eros of the Middle Ages loves (*agapa*) the soul, the ideal representation of the Beloved—they unite love with pious mysticism, religious ecstasy and womanly tenderness. Pale lovers with long braids stroll about, lifeless, without desire and without daring . . . Troubadors and bards elevate to the point of worship the instinct that pushes man toward woman, Don Quixotes chase nonexistent Dulcineas, and knights kneel before adored palace ladies, lone, wan, idle palace ladies who come and go proudly in the great halls of the Castles, without joy and without torment.

Gradually the Parthenon collapses and vulgar images and colors pollute the immaculate whiteness of its marble. And the mysticism and dreaming out in the West gives birth to and erects the Gothic temple. You feel that men do not enter such a temple with open, red hearts, and with tranquil upraised brows. God does not descend here—as he would have at another time in the marble sanctuary of the Parthenon. Man only bows here, overcome and on his knees, beseeching the Great One, the implacable punisher of sin... What hapless creatures, what beautiful women must have been on their knees on the cold tiles of these Gothic temples bewailing transgressions that Nature, the Great Goddess and Mother, forgives and justifies and imposes.

Gradually a kind of melancholy comes into being, an unnatural yearning for nonexistent worlds, a fear and dread anticipation of Hell, and of the tortures in the other life—the Second Coming approaches and souls tremble—prophets call wretched men to Repentance, the doors of the monasteries stand open wide, and terrified, pale mankind crams itself inside and waits. The fires of the Inquisition hideously illumine the night of the Middle Ages.

And that masterpiece of those years—Dante's poem—rises like a Gothic temple, pained, dark, and despairing.

In this night of the soul ancient Greece once again dawns, to enlighten and save. When the degenerate children of Byzantium were fleeing the Queen of Cities in defeat, carrying their diamonds and the icons of their saints with them, they also brought along Plato and Homer and Plutarch.

And the light illumines Italy and spills from the peaks into the dark plains, to open hearts and lips and thoughts. The mind is emancipated from Theology, Plato drives out Aristotle, the rhythm of the Renaissance rises grandly, Raphael drives out the pale Madonnas and reproduces his beloved Fornarina in the beautiful Madonnas and the gorgeous angels that now smile as they descend from the heavens, and you sense that they are coming down to give comfort...

95

Bacon and the Cartesian and Luther and Erasmus emancipate thought. Elegance is pursued in word and in manner and beautiful duchesses and marquises stroll about the throne, wanton at times, pretentious at times, but always beautiful.

The monarch grows more aristocratic each day. The court imitates the monarch. Everyone imitates the court.

The elite separate themselves from the people; the castles are encircled with huge moats.

The people are ignored, the nobility daily grows more arrogant, more licentious and degenerate.

There are signs of ferment. An infinite, tacit revolution grows audible—like muffled earthquake vibrations in the floor bedding of the people.

First man emancipates himself from theology.

He rebels against the excesses and simony of the clergy and loftily preaches reform. The Hussites fling themselves in the fire. No matter. In Wittenberg Luther burns the Pope's seal. The people were capable of understanding him. And Luther triumphs.

The first victory gives courage and confidence. Society, the classes, must be overturned. Progress bubbles inside the souls. The vibrations increase in frequency, beams of light glow from certain foreheads, a certain sun is expected, and all strain with impatient hearts toward the intellectual dawning of the world. And behold! magnificent, dreadful and redemptive, the souls' volcano explodes in France. All mankind glowed. Through blood and scaffold, with Danton and Robespierre and Marat in the lead, mankind advances toward freedom and light. Equal all. For once man becomes aware of his rights and his mission and his worth. The night of August 26 illumined the world. The bourgeois won their first victory. Why should they not dare like this always? *Dare and you shall succeed.* And the cages that exist in the soul of every man open, and the passions are freed and so is ambition and the lust for power, and the joy of conquest, and the gratification of victory through whatever means. *Quo non ascendam?* The hero of the modern age is not the nobleman, not the highborn, not the pale, degenerate aristocrat of the drawing room, but the man, the youth, who is shut in his office or stooped over his book studying and writing, he's the fellow out there who is shouting and working and fighting and winning.

There is no limit to his desires, no respite. The person who buckles under in the struggle of life falls in a heap on the ground and is trampled by the myriad others who are rushing behind him. There are no barriers. The goal is self-interest, the goal sanctifies the means. Self-interest is called glory or wealth or power. It doesn't matter. The man of the modern age knows no limits. He thinks he is capable of becoming whatever he desires. And what doesn't nineteenth-century man desire! Nietzsche in philosophy, Bismarck in politics, are the two great, the two invincible prophets of the deification of the self.

How is it possible for gods to exist, shouts Nietzsche, when I, myself, am not a God? Therefore gods do not exist.

There is only one God, exclaims Richepin, me!

From the simplicity and joy of antiquity, from the devotion and ecstasy and faith of the Middle Ages, we have ended up in the licentiousness of thought of modern times.

Everything has veered, everything is in flux. We find ourselves in a transitional age, in a nervous century. The soul does not know where to anchor itself. An infinite earthquake shakes our convictions. We are unable to love the things our fathers loved. They're phantoms. All the fears and hopes of our forebears are chimeras. Faith, love, morality, devotion, virtue, all are tottering.

The beautiful corpse of the Nazarene was buried—not many years ago—in the cemetery where the dead gods rest.

The critic implacably stoops and examines. Implacable anatomist of the ideal, he stoops and examines: Religion is a beautiful illusion, a beautiful world, but nonexistent. Love, a common and childish instinct, a chemical attraction of bodies, as Goethe said. Innocence, a pretense or stupidity. Woman, neither better nor worse than man—impossible. Friendship is nonexistent. Politics, the great corrupter of character, is a triumph of the treacherous and the base and the crafty . . . everything, everything, has been exposed. And in every soul disgust heaves like a wave from a quagmire and extinguishes the great candles of joy and peace and innocence.

And in the debris of all these souls—the seed that Christianity had sown waxed strong in us and the sickness of the age blossomed.

And the breed of moderns was born: Werther, Faust, Manfred, René. Werther, the sentimental and melancholy suicide. Faust, the insatiable, the constantly yearning. Gigantic revolutionary Manfred, rising like a titan asking toward what end he was sent and why was he sent. "When I see the world around me, in which I appear as nothing," says Byron, the greatest victim of the sickness of the age, "thoughts come to me that could, I suspect, hold sway throughout the entire world."

In vain René hides his melancholy in the forests of America.

Sickened, the greatest brows of the century stoop and ponder. Wounded, the most beautiful souls leave the palaestra.[4] Their pain becomes a song and mankind in their midst, also weary, gathers round them and listens: they sing of the brow's sorrow and incurable pain.

Not a single enticement is left. We know everything. The sun of truth pierced all those morning specters, all the mist with the beautiful shapes and the delightful curves of nonexistent bodies. We have exposed everything. Zephyros is no longer Chloe's lover, the enamored Moon no longer seeks Endymion on earth. Our springs and forests no longer hide Naiads and Dryads. "Illusion is transitory and pain is eternal." We know what women's lips give and why virgins' cheeks blush and we know all the animalistic secrets of the nuptial bed and nighttime love.

The manner in which man develops today is prodigious. He knows at a very early age what old men of past generations never knew. While still young he has grown pale over volumes of books and has become poisoned with the great desires and enormous thirst of the modern soul.... How can anyone today understand the simple joy of one's forebears?

We have grown weary of the wisdom of books, poets come and go and leave us their tears and their doubts, and we have wearied of reading and inquiring and waiting for answers.

Who can love, today, in the grand manner of his forefathers, joyfully like his ancestors, after having seen in sated detail all the mysteries of love in the books and psychological analyses of modern writers?

When her lips come close to mine I know—they told me—what she is thinking, what orgies are forming under her skin.

When I go to Church I know—they told me—what is hiding in the holy Chalice, what the eyes of the priests are thinking, and why men go and why women go.

The man of today knows everything. They left nothing virginal in our soul. Power, Science, glory, no longer suffice for us. We seek something else. "Beyond good and evil" some mystery pulls us.

The great souls of the modern age are restless.

They are degenerate and corrupt. The Edgar Poes and the Alfred de Mussets abandon themselves to drink. The Oscar Wildes fall into depravity, the Baudelaires and Huysmans revel in their licentious passions, the Swifts and the

Nietzsches and the Guy de Maupassants abandon themselves to travel and women and die insane, the Thomas de Quincys wallow in their hashish.

Neither peace nor happiness will ever again smile in the depraved-by-knowledge soul of modern man.

Why do men throw themselves into travel today, and traverse the world and the seas and die in the deserts? It is the restlessness of the modern soul.

It is the absence of serenity in the paternal home, where the aged parents lived and died tranquil and unshaken. All the sentiments have grown perverted, they've joined forces with blood, with depravity, with madness, in order to make up something new, some unknown pleasure, to sate the hunger of the modern soul. Remember the sadists and the masochists and the fetishists who mix blood and idolotry with love. It is the profound sickness of the modern age, the *mal du siècle,* the great epidemic in the delicate, weary, aristocratic souls.

"We are nothing," says Psiharis,[5] "we are nothing, neither strong arms, nor upheld heads, merely wounded, tired feet."

We are nothing but wounded, tired feet. A hard inflexible Doom bears down on our brow. Man's soul resembles the wretched Oedipus of old. You remember his anguish and agony to learn—to learn who he is, what crime he has committed, what woman he has in his bed. He begins to presage, he begins to shudder at the prospect of his confrontation with truth, and yet he does not stop. He proceeds, pale and speechless and seeks to learn everything... Everything. And he learned and was blinded.

Our soul resembles Oedipus. Throughout the ages our soul has played out nothing else but Sophocles' tragedy: *Oedipus Tyrannus.*

Joyful and serene at the start—a sovereign in the world. He knows nothing—he is fortunate. Such was Oedipus in the first act. Little by little, from a few allusions, from a few imprudent words dropped by the woman, he begins to doubt, to forebode a bit, to inquire, to feel distressed. The soul is in the second act, of doubt, inquiry, curiosity, hesitation.

The great men, the Tiresians, unveil the truth. But the soul shudders at the terrible revelation and continues to doubt. And sends out investigators everywhere and inquires more vigorously and penetrates deeper and drives away the deceiving hopes, and finally we find ourselves in the last act —it sees the truth and is blinded. There is neither joy nor pleasure any longer. We know what awaits us. After the grave, nothing. Maybe there is a God, but what does it matter to us as long as we're meant to die, as long as the skeletons are bedded inconsolable in the earth. There is neither joy nor rest anymore. The excessive light blinded our souls.

We stoop under the weight of all the dead generations' disillusioned. They banished us from the palaces of hope and we run to foreign lands and curse Apollo and futilely grope in the dark to find the tender hand of an Antigone. Maybe Antigone is Faith. Maybe Antigone is Love. Maybe Antigone is Science.

If she is Faith, Antigone has died. If she is Love, she has grown corrupt and become a whore and leads the poor blind wretch into lairs and brothels, or into lying, nonexistent consolations. . . .

If Antigone is Science, and only Science, then she is no consolation, and her hand is no longer tender and compassionate. It is an iron, heavy hand that supports but drags without pity—without pity because it is almighty—down there where all hopes and ideals are snuffed out. Science, the merciless daughter of our mind, drags her wretched father toward the infinite sorrow that all souls understand when they perceive that after death there is nothing, absolutely nothing.

Karma Nirvami

Pinakothiki, March-April-May, 1906

Notes

1. N. K. received his Doctor of Law degree from the University of Athens on December 9, 1906.

2. *Report to Greco,* trans. P. A. Bien (New York: Simon and Schuster, 1965), chap. 15, Athens.

3. Theriso was the site in western Crete where Eleutherios Venizelos (1864-1936), the then Cretan councillor and later prime minister of Greece, proclaimed the union of Crete with Greece on April 20, 1905. The Cretan Venizelos, one of the great heroes of Crete, and indeed of all Greece, was instrumental not only in uniting Crete with mainland Greece but also in establishing Greece as a modern member in the world of nations. Gavriilidis's parallel with the young Kazantzakis proved prophetic.

4. Psiloritis, the highest point in the central range of mountains in Crete is also known by its ancient name, Ida.

5. *Katharevousa* is the official language of Greece, used in government, schools, courts of law, and until recently, in most of the media. It is a cultivated artificial tongue rooted in Attic Greek and the Hellenistic *Koine,* and has among its supporters the educated middle class, conservatives, aristocrats, and pedants, who see in it the opportunity to preserve and revive the archaic Greek language. Greece's "spoken" language is the *demotiki,* or vulgar tongue of the people, a rich language also rooted in a Greek history of several millennia, but pliable and still evolving. It is the favored language of modern Greek poets, writers, liberals, and intellectuals. For analysis of the Greek language, see Kimon Friar's section on Language and Literature in his Introduction to *Modern Greek Poetry* (New York: Simon and Schuster, 1973), pp. 6-13; see also Peter Bien's *Kazantzakis and the Linguistic Revolution in Greek Literature* (Princeton, N. J.: Princeton University Press, 1972).

6. Demotic. See n. 5.

7. In his review upon its recent reemergence in Athens, Kimon Friar describes *Serpent and Lily* as a novella par excellence of decadence,

worthy of taking its place among the *fin-de-siècle* writers throughout Europe, having all the characteristics of that school. The Friar review appeared in *The Athenian* (Athens) May 1, 1976. *Serpent and Lily* was republished in Greece in 1974.

8. *The Sickness of the Age* (in this edition).

9. See also Kimon Friar's analyses in his Introduction to *The Odyssey: a Modern Sequel* (New York: Simon and Schuster, 1958), (cited as *Odyssey* in text), and *The Saviors of God: Spiritual Exercises* (New York: Simon and Schuster, 1960) (hereafter cited as *Spiritual Exercises*).

10. *The Sickness of the Age.*

11. The reader may want to also consider "for love is strong as death," and "jealousy is cruel as the grave," in *Song of Solomon* (8.6). In the context of Kazantzakis's frequent use of imagery from that biblical poem, perhaps a word here is in order on the theme of Love and Death in both works, the "twin realities" which Marvin H. Pope in his book *Song of Songs* (Garden City, N.Y.: Doubleday, 1977) asserts haunt every sentient soul. The coupling together of Love and Death in the *Serpent and Lily* story invites comparison with Professor Pope's modern interpretation of *Song of Songs* (pictorially illustrated by the sepulchral love scene on the book's cover based on a fourth century B.C. Etruscan sarcophagos), which suggests that the correlation between Love and Death is that ancient love poem's immortal message.

12. *Spiritual Exercises.*

13. The opening sentence to the Prologue of *Spiritual Exercises.*

14. The Prologue to *Spiritual Exercises.*

15. Crete, August 18, 1921.

16. Helen Kazantzakis, *Nikos Kazantzakis: A Biography Based on His Letters,* trans. Amy Mims (New York: Simon and Schuster, 1968), p. 77.

17. *Symposium,* trans. Theodora Vasils and Themi Vasils (New York: Thomas Y. Crowell, 1975).

18. *Journeying,* trans. Themi Vasils and Theodora Vasils (Boston: Little, Brown, 1975).

19. Kazantzakis was fond of referring to the twenty-four letters of the Greek alphabet as soldiers to be enlisted in the struggle against mortality. "Words! Words! There is no other salvation! I have nothing in my power but twenty-four little lead soldiers. I will mobilize. I will raise an army. I will conquer death!" (*Journeying,* Prologue, p. 6).

20. "What saved [Kazantzakis] from the alienated, curiously uninformed fate of most intellectuals today were his roots in the very old—his roots in both Classical and Byzantine Greek thought and art. Indeed, he could grasp the new more confidently and more responsibly because of his

instinctive rootedness in the old. His inherited sense of humanity, as well as his artistic vitality, protected him from both the harshness and purposelessness to which modern ideology is prone...." George Anastaplo, *Human Being and Citizen: Essays on Virtue, Freedom and the Common Good* (Chicago: Swallow Press, 1975), p. 253.

21. See *Report to Greco*, chap. 31, The Cretan Glance.

22. *The Odyssey: A Modern Sequel.*

23. Pandelis Prevelakis, *Nikos Kazantzakis and His Odyssey: A Study of the Poet and the Poem*, trans. Philip Sherrard (New York: Simon and Schuster, 1961). Prevelakis was a young student when he met Kazantzakis in 1926. There developed a friendship between them based on mutual respect and admiration, which lasted a lifetime.

24. I am indebted to Adele Bloch for these observations in her "Dual Masks of Kazantzakis," *Journal of Modern Literature*, vol. 2, no. 2 (1971-1972). It should be noted that most, if not all, of N. K.'s flights to monasteries occurred in the earlier period of his life, during the years (1914-1924) of domestic difficulties. His frequent travels and ascetic retreats were often prompted by a need for escape, as well as his need for the monastic solitude that would allow him to write in peace.

25. See Epilogue, *Report to Greco*. In his confession to his "grandfather," Kazantzakis, with characteristic restraint in matters private, lifts the veil just enough to allow the reader a fleeting glimpse of his personal regard for the women he has known: "Women I loved. I was fortunate in chancing to meet extraordinary women along my route. No man ever did me so much good or aided my struggle so greatly as these women—and one above all, the last. But over this love-smitten body I throw the veil which the sons of Noah threw over their drunken father. I like our ancestors' myth about Eros and Psyche; . . . it is both shameful and dangerous to light a lamp, dispel the darkness, and see two bodies locked in an embrace. You knew this, you who hid your beloved helpmate Jeronima. Intrepid fellow athlete, cool fountain in our inhuman solitude, great comfort!. . . poverty and nakedness are nothing, provided you have a good wife. We had good wives; yours was named Jeronima, mine Helen. How many times did we not say to ourselves as we looked at them, Blessed the day we were born! But we did not allow women, even the dearest, to lead us astray. We did not follow their flower-strewn road; we took them with us. No, we did not take them, these dauntless companions followed our ascents of their own free will." (El Greco, the Cretan-born Domenicos Theotokopulos, was born in Fodhele, a short distance from N. K.'s native Irakleion in 1548(?); N. K. saw in him a kindred spirit and adopted him as his "grandfather.")

26. Helen Kazantzakis, *Nikos Kazantzakis,* p. 368.

27. In *Nikephoros Phokas.*

28. In *Christ.*

29. In the *Odyssey.*

30. Kazantzakis attributed his dual vision to his double ancestral root. He claimed twin currents of blood ran through his veins, Bedouin from his father, and Greek from his mother. His Bedouin kinship he liked to imagine came from his paternal ancestors who had put down roots in the village of Barbari near Irakleion, an Arab settlement that traced its lineage as far back as the eleventh century when the Byzantine Emperor Nikephoros Phokas came to Crete and freed the island from its Arab conquerers. His mother came from Greek peasant stock "whose endurance and sweetness were of the earth itself." Both parents, he claimed, were clearly manifested in his hands; the right being very strong, masculine and completely lacking in sensitivity, and the left excessively, even pathologically, sensitive (*Report to Greco,* chap. 4, The Son).

31. W. B. Stanford, *The Ulysses Theme* (New York: Barnes and Noble, 1968).

32. *Report to Greco,* chap. 16, Return to Crete.

33. *Zorba the Greek,* trans. Carl Wildman (New York: Simon and Schuster, 1964), the first of the great novels that was started during the third period. See the accompanying Bibliography for some of the principal works of Nikos Kazantzakis from 1906-1957.

34. *Report to Greco,* chap. 31, The Cretan Glance.

SERPENT AND LILY

1. *Kerameikos,* the site of the most important Athenian cemetery of antiquity, bordering the city walls not far from the Acropolis, served as the starting point for the great Panathenaic processions that were part of the annual festivals honoring the Goddess Athena. (See nn. 2, 7).

2. The Double Gates (Dipylon) through which the Panathenaic procession passed, and the Sacred Gate through which the Eleusinian and Dionysian worshipers passed, were situated in the Kerameikos district, the latter gate opening on the Sacred Road that led to Eleusis, and the former (Dipylon) main gate of the city, receiving the greatest volume of ancient traffic to and from Piraeus and Boeotia. The Kerameikos Cemetery lay outside the Dipylon and extended on either side of the two main adjoining roads. Cemeteries existed in this district since at least the twelfth century B.C. The City Wall which was built in the seventh century B.C. sepa-

rated the Kerameikos district in two, creating an Outer Kerameikos and an Inner Kerameikos, the latter becoming the site where potters and smiths established themselves, thus giving rise to the speculation that the potters gave Kerameikos its name. Pausanius attributes the district's name to the hero Keramos, supposed son of Dionysos and Ariadne. The area between the Sacred and Dipylon gates, in addition to serving as the starting point for the great ritual processions, also was the site of the *Pompeion,* the storehouse where all the vehicles and equipment of the great festivals were stored.

3. The Acropolis, the rocky hill at Athens dedicated to the city's patron goddess Athena Parthenos upon which her temple stands, is often referred to as the Sacred Rock.

4. Nike is a secondary divinity representing Victory in Greek mythology. The statue of Athena Parthenos which stood in the core of the Parthenon held a diminutive statue of Nike, the winged goddess of Victory in her right hand. The colossal statue of the virgin goddess (parthenos) whom Kazantzakis's hero-lover invokes in this story, stood 39 feet high on its pedestal within the sanctuary. At the goddess' feet was a shield portraying the battle of the Amazons and the Athenians, and at the base of her shield a serpent. The face, hands, and feet of the statue were of ivory, and the pupils of the eyes were of precious stones. The dress and other ornaments were of gold and all were presumably designed by Phidias to glow in a kind of awesome mystery in the shadowy interior of the temple, whose only illumination came through the open doorway.

5. The Metopes on the south side of the Parthenon depict the battle of the Lapiths and the Centaurs. According to legend, the Centaurs which are portrayed throughout Greek mythology as half man and half horse, were invited by the Lapith king, Pirithous, to the marriage of his daughter. At the feast the Centaurs, emboldened by wine, insulted their hosts by forcing their attentions on the bride and other guests, thus setting off the celebrated battle of the Lapiths and Centaurs, a battle scene frequently depicted in Greek art as representative of Civilization versus Barbarism.

6. Phidias was the Athenian sculptor famed for the decorating of the Parthenon.

7. Athenian maidens of the aristocracy, called *kanephoroi* (basket bearers) were part of the annual ceremonial processions that paid tribute to the city's patron goddess. The Propylaea was the monumental entrance hall at the top of the Acropolis through which they passed on their way to the ritual shrine. This occurred every August, the designated anniversary date of the birth of Athena. (Today in Greece annual homage is paid on

August 15 to the Virgin Mary, protectress of the Christian faithful. This holy day commemorating the Assumption of the Virgin Mary is one of the most important in the Greek Orthodox Church.) The festival honoring Athena was celebrated with exceptional pomp and splendor every fourth year. This special celebration, called the Panathenaea, lasted four days and was essentially an event in which the Athenians offered homage and presents to their goddess, the most important of which was the embroidered *peplos,* the ritual gift that had been woven to drape an earlier wooden *Xoanon,* the primitive wooden statue of Athena Polias that was housed in the Erechtheum. This *peplos* was borne in state in a procession as depicted in the Ionic frieze on the outside of the Parthenon (the major sculptures of which are now in the British Museum among the "Elgin Marbles") composed of the city's notables who assembled at the Kerameikos and set out with ceremonial splendor from the *Pompeion,* making their way through the streets of Athens to the Acropolis. Leading the procession was a wagonlike ship with the *peplos* presumably spread over it like a sail. Following the wagonship were the noble ladies (*ergastenai*) who had worked on the *peplos,* and the *kanephoroi,* the maidens who carried the festival's sacred objects. Behind them came other leading personages, followed by the sacrificers with their animals. At the rear of the procession came a splendid cavalcade of army units. The wagonship stopped at the foot of the Acropolis as the slope was too steep for wheels, and the procession continued the climb to the top on foot. Although the great procession was the main event, the festivities also included competitions in the arts and in athletics. The victors were awarded olive oil harvested from the olive trees sacred to the goddess in special victors' urns called Panathenaic amphorae.

8. Salamis is the tiny crescent-shaped island off the coast of Attica in the Saronic Gulf in whose straights one of the decisive battles of the world, the famous Battle of Salamis, was fought (September 22(?), 480 B.C.). It was here that the small Greek ships destroyed the vast Persian fleet under the eyes of Xerxes himself who had set up a silver throne on the rocky crest of Aigaleos overlooking Salamis to watch the battle. Salamis henceforth became a symbol of victory for the Greeks who with this battle turned the tide against the Persian plan of conquest.

9. Hebe in Greek mythology was the lovely cup-bearer for the Olympian gods with whom she dwelled on the summit of Mount Olympos in Thessaly. As the Goddess of Youth, she served in the great palace of Zeus where they all dined on ambrosia and nectar that the young cup-bearer passed among the gods.

10. Sophocles' chorus sings of the flowers of Kolonos in Oedipus Colo-

neus. It is the hilly site near the Kerameikos where Oedipus found refuge.

11. The mountain range Hymettos, extending along the southeast extremity of the Attic plain is famed for its honey and marble.

12. The Karyatides are the six maidens who stand in the place of the customary supporting columns of the south portico of the Erechtheum on the Acropolis.

13. In translating this quotation I took into consideration the King James interpretation of the Song of Solomon.

14. The Aphrodite of Cnidos, named after the ancient Dorian city that was founded in the early Iron Age in Asia Minor, was the celebrated statue by Praxiteles which stood in the Temple of Aphrodite at Cnidos. The sculpture is said to have caused a scandal in its day because of the unorthodox way in which it was rendered. Its style departed from the majestic austerity that, until then, characterized the statues of divinities and was molded in a freer more sensuous manner. Particularly objectionable was the complete nudity of the goddess and the almost palpable fleshlike appearance of the marble. While Greeks were accustomed to nudity in courtesans, they objected to seeing such freedom taken with a goddess. Despite the seeming irreverence, the Cnidian Aphrodite eventually became the most imitated statue of the Hellenic and Roman worlds. (See also n. 15 following).

15. Phryne, the beloved of Praxiteles and one of the most famous courtesans of ancient Greece, is rumored to have been the model for the Praxiteles statue of the Cnidian Aphrodite. There is a story about her that she had once stood trial in Athens on a charge of impiety. In his defense of her before the judges, Hyperides, the legend goes, relied on the exquisite beauty of her body to win his case. Bringing her before her accusers, he ripped the chiton from her body and turning to the judges, appealed to their aesthetic appreciation—and the charges against her were dropped.

16. A biblical reference to the mountain where it is believed the Law was given to Moses.

17. Here Kazantzakis's imagery draws on the earlier, more remote predecessor of Aphrodite, the ancient Phoenician Astarte, goddess of beauty and sexual love. This goddess of Semitic antiquity was believed to be endowed with the reproductive powers that brought together all living things, humans as well as fowls and beasts, in the act of procreating love.

18. Aphrodite was worshiped in Greece in two different manifestations: Aphrodite Ouranos, the chaste heavenly goddess of higher pure love, and Aphrodite Pandemos, the earthy popular goddess of sensual lust.

19. This multilevel reference to Galatea, with its inverted symbolism,

draws on the legend of Pygmalion, the Cypriot sculptor who, having despaired of ever finding a woman who could meet his impossible ideal, resorted to creating one out of ivory, and so he sculpted a maiden of such perfection that he fell in love with her and prayed to Aphrodite to bring her to life. The patron goddess of Love and Beauty, the legend goes, could not deny him his plea and she imbued his ivory statue with life. In earlier Greek mythology Galatea was the Nereïd daughter born in the sea to Nereus and Doris, offspring of Pantos and Okeanos. Hesiod in Theogony (245) describes her beauty as great even among goddesses.

20. This ancient sinister boatman of the nether world who ferried the dead across the river Acheron, is synonymous in the modern Greek tongue with death. Charon's anthropomorphic essence invokes a more physical and personal image than the word *thanatos,* somewhat like the Grim Reaper in English tradition.

21. Bacchantes date back to an early period of orgiastic Dionysian rites. They were the female followers (Maenads) of the god of the vine and their name is synonymous with wild wantoness and unrestraint. At the peak of their ritualistic revelries, urged on by the shrill music of the flute and clash of cymbals, their ecstasies were said to reach such a pitch that they would run wild through the forests, waving burning brands and Thyrsoi (ritual wands) and would tear apart the young of wild animals and eat the raw flesh.

22. In Greek mythology Ouranos the Sky, and husband of Gaia the Earth, sired several children, the last of which was Chronos who castrated his father Ouranos with a sickle and thus ended his reign.

23. Ashtoreth is another name for Astarte, the goddess of sexual love (see n. 17).

24. Priapos was the god of male generative power.

25. The aeolian lyre was an ancient musical instrument of stretched strings that produced a sound similar to that of the winds, taking its name from Aeolos, the guardian of the winds.

26. The terrible death agony of Laocoön is immortalized in the Rhodian sculpture grouping of the first century B.C. now in the Vatican museum. It depicts Laocoön trying to rescue his two sons while all three are being mangled by two giant serpents, a punishment ordained by Athena whose wrath Laocoön incurred for warning the Trojans against accepting the wooden horse of the Greeks.

27. Shunammite, also referred to as Shulammite in Song of Songs, evokes the fair maiden from Shunem (earlier Shula) in ancient Palestine who became the beloved of Solomon.

1. This figurative passage showing Socrates moving with ease from the physical to the metaphysical, from gymnasium to Academy to lofty Mount Ida (ancient birthplace of Zeus, and symbolic sanctuary of the spirit), is presumably drawn from Plato's dialogue *The Laws,* in which a Cretan, a Spartan and an Athenian (resembling Socrates) discourse on the laws while walking from Knossos to the god's domain.

2. The Greeks rarely drank wine in the pure state; it was mixed with water in a large urn called a *krater,* and ladled into clay cups from which it was drunk.

3. Numerous references to the *hetairai* (courtesans, literally meaning companions or friends) of Greece are made by Herodotus and Athenaeus. Xenophon, too, in *Memorabilia III 11,* describes an amusing account of Socrates in conversation with the famed courtesan Theodota. These courtesans were often intelligent, cultivated women who delighted men with their wit as well as their body. Many were talented musicians and dancers who would also perform at banquets. Most, however, were slaves or women from the poorer classes. Some, like Phryne and Rhodopis, managed glorious immortality in monuments of marble and stone. Some of the more exceptional even achieved brilliant marriages—such a one allegedly was Aspasia, the celebrated mistress of Pericles who eventually became his consort. The practice of prostitution, both in the service of religion (by consecrated priestesses) and as a means of livelihood (by *hetairai*), was customary in ancient Greece, as in many ancient countries.

4. The palaestra was the gymnasium of ancient Greeks, the name deriving from *pale,* or wrestling, which was one of the five exercises required in the pentathlon.

5. John Psiharis (1854-1929) was a Greek writer who touched off a controversy in the 1880s with his publications calling for the abolition of the pseudo-classical language of the Athenian elite known as purist or *katharevousa,* and advocated the adoption of the *demotiki* (see n. 5 in Notes on Introduction). He helped shape the course of future modern Greek poetry.

Selected Bibliography

Note: An asterisk indicates the works available in English translation. The letters following each citation are as follows: D, drama; E, essay or article; N, novel; P, poetry; T, travel articles; Tr, translation. (The date in the left-hand column indicates the year the work was written.)

PRINCIPAL WORKS OF NIKOS KAZANTZAKIS

1906 *Serpent and Lily.* Trans. Theodora Vasils. Berkeley, Los Angeles, London: University of California Press, 1980. (N)

1906 *The Sickness of the Age.* Trans. Theodora Vasils. Berkeley, Los Angeles, London: University of California Press, 1980. (E)

1906 *Day is Breaking.* Produced in 1907, published in part. *Pinakothiki* (August 1907), and *Nea Estia,* 63 (May 15, 1958), 746-749. (D)

1907-1908 "Letters from Paris." Republished in *Nea Estia,* 64 (August 15, 1958), 1208-1215; 64 (September 1, 1958), 1284-1288. (T)

1908 *Broken Souls.* Published serially. *O Noumas* (August 30, 1909-February 7, 1910). (N)

1908 "Friedrich Nietzsche's Philosophy of Law and the State," reprinted in *Kainouria Epochē* (Summer 1959), pp. 34-89. (E)

1909 *The Masterbuilder. Panathenea* (1910). (D)

1909 *Comedy: A Tragedy in One Act.* Trans. Kimon Friar. *The Literary Review,* 18, 4 (Summer 1975). Produced at the University of Michigan, 1972. (D)

1909 "Science Has Gone Bankrupt," *Panathenea,* 19 (November 15, 1909), 71-75; *Nea Estia,* 64 (September 15, 1958), 1374-1378. (E)

1909 "The Demoticists' Society 'Solomos' of Irakleion, Crete." *O Noumas,* 347 (June 7, 1909), 9-12. (E)

1910-1915 Translations as follows: William James, *The Theory of Emotion;* Nietzsche, *The Birth of Tragedy;* Nietzsche, *Thus Spake Zarathustra;* Eckermann, *Conversations with Goethe;* Laisant, *Education*

113

on a Scientific Basis; Maeterlinck, Le Trésor des Humbles; Darwin, On the Origin of Species; Buchner, Power and Matter; Bergson, Laughter; Plato, Alcibiades 1, Alcibiades 2; Plato, Ion-Minos-Demodocus-Sisyphus-Cleitophon. Athens: George Phexis.

1912? "H. Bergson." Kainouria Epochē, III (1958), 12-30. (E)

1915? Nikephoros Phokas. See Theatro: Tragedies with Byzantine Themes. Athens: Diphros, 1956. (D)

1915? Odysseas. See Theatro: Tragedies with Ancient Themes. Athens: Diphros, 1955. (D)

1915? Christ. See Theatro: Tragedies with Byzantine Themes. Athens: Diphros, 1956. (D)

1920-1924 Letters to Galatea published in English translation as: *Selected Letters to Galatea and to Papastephanou. Trans. Philip Ramp and Katerina Rooke. New York: Caratzas, 1979.

1922 *Symposium. Trans. Theodora Vasils and Themi Vasils. New York: Thomas Y. Crowell; Minerva Press, 1975. (E)

1923 *The Saviors of God: Spiritual Exercises. Trans. Kimon Friar. New York: Simon and Schuster, 1960. (E)

1924 Odyssey, first draft of Books 1-6. (P)

1924-1925 "Confession of Faith." Nea Ephemeris (February 26, 1925). (E)

1925 Travel articles on Russia. Eleutheros Logos (November-December, 1925). (T)

1926 *Journeying. Travel articles on Italy, Egypt, Sinai, Jerusalem, and Cyprus. Trans. Themi Vasils and Theodora Vasils. Boston: Little, Brown, 1975. (T)

1927 "Rosa Luxemburg." Ilysia (May 22, 1927), pp. 12-15. (E)

1927 Odyssey, first draft of Books 7-24. (P)

1927 "Impressions of Soviet Russia," Proia (from January 8, 1928, on). (T)

1928 (Revision of Spiritual Exercises).

1928 "What is Happening in Russia," Anagennisi (January, 1928), pp. 193-198). (Speech)

1929 *Toda Raba. Trans. Amy Mims. New York: Simon and Schuster, 1964. (N)

1929 Odyssey, second draft. (P)

1930 "History of Russian Literature," Vol. A, Eleutherudakis (1930). (E)

1930 "History of Russian Literature," Vol. B, Eleutherudakis (1930). (E)

1930-1931 Children's books. Athens: Dimitrakos, 1931. (T)

1930-1931 One half of French-Greek dictionary.

1930-1931 *"Confession of Faith," expanded version. See Nikos Kazantzakis: A Biography. Trans. Amy Mims. New York: Simon and Schuster, 1968, pp. 565-570. (E)

1932 Dante, *Divine Comedy*. *Kyklos* (1934). (Tr)

1932-1937 *Terzinas* (published in a collected edition). Athens, 1960. (P)

1933 *Spain*. Trans. Amy Mims. New York: Simon and Schuster, 1963. (T)

1933 *Contemporary Spanish Lyrical Poetry* (includes J. R. Jimenez, Antonio Machado, Miguel de Unamuno, Pedro Salinas, Moreno Villa, Federico Garcia Lorca, Rafael Alberti, Vicente Alexandre, Manuel Altolaguirre, Concha Mendez Cuesta, Ernestina de Champourcin), *Kyklos* (April, May, June, August, September, 1933). (Tr)

1935 *Japan-China*. Trans. George C. Pappageotes. New York: Simon and Schuster, 1963. (T)

1936 *The Rock Garden*. Trans. Richard Howard. New York: Simon and Schuster, 1963. (N)

1936 Pirandello. *Questa Sera Si Recita A Soggetto* (for Athens Royal Theater). (Tr)

1936 Goethe, *Faust* (Part One). *Kathimerini* (March 8-July 5, 1937). (Tr)

1936 "Fear and Hunger," *Kathimerini* (July 20, 1936). (E)

1936 "What I Saw for Forty Days in Spain," *Kathimerini* (November 24, 1936-January 17, 1937). (T)

1937 *Othello Returns*. (D)

1937 *Journey to the Morea*. Trans. F. A. Reed. New York: Simon and Schuster, 1965. (T)

1937 *Melissa*. See *Three Plays*. Trans. Athena Gianakas Dallas. New York: Simon and Schuster, 1969. (D)

1938 *The Odyssey: A Modern Sequel*. Trans. Kimon Friar. New York: Simon and Schuster, 1958. (P)

1939 *Julian the Apostate*. See *Theatro: Tragedies with Byzantine Themes*. Athens: Diphros, 1956. (D)

1940 *England*. Trans. Amy Mims. New York: Simon and Schuster, 1966. (T)

1941 *Buddha* (first draft). (D)

1941 *Life and Times of Alexis Zorba* (first draft). (N)

1942 Homer, *Iliad* (with Professor I. Th. Kakridis). Athens, 1955. (Tr)

1943 *Buddha* (second draft). See *Theatro: Tragedies with Various Themes*. Athens: Diphros, 1956. (D)

1943 *Zorba the Greek* (*Life and Times of Alexis Zorba*). Trans. Carl Wildman. New York: Simon and Schuster, 1964. (N)

1943 *Prometheus the Fire-Bringer: Prometheus Bound: Prometheus Unbound*. See *Theatro: Tragedies with Ancient Themes*. Athens: Diphros, 1955. (D)

1943 Jens Johannes Jorgensen. *Saint Francis*. (Tr)

1943-1944 Homer. Odyssey (with Professor Kakridis). Reworked 1956-1957; completed by Professor Kakridis after N. K.'s death. Athens. (Tr)

1944 *Kapodistrias.* Athens: Alikioti, 1946. (D)

1944 *Constantine Palaiologos.* See *Theatro: Tragedies with Byzantine Themes.* Athens: Diphros, 1956. (D)

1948 *Sodom and Gomorrah.* See *Theatro: Tragedies with Various Themes.* Athens: Diphros, 1956. Trans. Kimon Friar. *The Literary Review,* XIX, 2 (Winter 1976). (Produced at the Jan Hus Playhouse in New York City 1963 under the title of *Burn Me to Ashes*). (D)

1948 *The Greek Passion (Christ Recrucified).* Trans. Jonathan Griffin. New York: Simon and Schuster, 1959. (N)

1949 *The Fratricides.* Trans. Athena Gianakas Dallas. New York: Simon and Schuster, 1964. (N)

1949 *Kouros.* See *Three Plays.* Trans. Athena Gianakas Dallas. New York: Simon and Schuster, 1969. (D)

1949 *Christopher Columbus.* See *Three Plays.* Trans. Athena Gianakas Dallas. New York: Simon and Schuster, 1969. (D)

1949-1950 *Freedom or Death (Kapetan Mihalis).* Trans. Jonathan Griffin. New York: Simon and Schuster, 1955. (N)

1950-1951 *The Last Temptation of Christ.* Trans. P. A. Bien. New York: Simon and Schuster, 1960. (N)

1953 *Saint Francis (God's Little Pauper).* Trans. P. A. Bien. New York: Simon and Schuster, 1962. (N)

1955-1956 *Report to Greco.* Trans. P. A. Bien. New York: Simon and Schuster, 1965. (Autobiography)

1902-1957 *Letters.* See Helen Kazantzakis, *Nikos Kazantzakis: A Biography.* Trans. Amy Mims. New York: Simon and Schuster, 1968.

1926-1957 Letters. See P. Prevelakis, *Four Hundred Letters of Kazantzakis to Prevelakis.* Athens, 1965.

For additional information, see Peter Bien (Columbia Essays on Modern Writers, *Nikos Kazantzakis* [New York: Columbia University Press, 1972], G. K. Katsimbalis (*Bibliographia N. Kazantzaki, A' 1906-1948* [Athens]), and Pandelis Prevelakis (*Nikos Kazantzakis and his Odyssey: A Study of the Poet and the Poem* [New York: Simon and Schuster, 1961], Notes).

ABOUT THE AUTHOR

Nikos Kazantzakis was born in Irakleion, Crete, on February 18, 1883. He received a law degree from the University of Athens and continued his studies, primarily in philosophy and literature, in Europe. Travel was essential to his education and he spent alternating periods of his life away from his native Greece, writing and traveling throughout Europe and the East. He earned the acclaim of his peers as one of the great European writers of the twentieth century and was repeatedly nominated for the Nobel Prize. Among his numerous works are novels, dramas, essays, travel journals, philosophical works, and translations, but he is perhaps best known in the United States for his novels, *Zorba the Greek,* and *The Greek Passion* (made into a film, *He Who Must Die*). He died in Freiburg, Germany, on October 26, 1957.

ABOUT THE TRANSLATOR

Theodora Vasils, a native-born American, has co-translated with Themi Vasils Nikos Kazantzakis's *Journeying* (Little, Brown and Company, 1975), and *Symposium* (Thomas Y. Crowell Company, 1975). Among her translations are short stories published in various literary journals, and a book of poetry, *In Another Light,* by Koralia Theotoka (Ikaros Publishing Co., Athens). Her work has been cited in the *Encyclopaedia Britannica,* Greece 323 (15th edition, 1977 printing). In progress, the work of the contemporary Greek writer, Elli Nezeriti.